THE MONUMENTS CLUB: LAVA RIVER CAVE

Published by
Heritage Publishing. US
Bradenton, Florida

THE MONUMENTS CLUB: LAVA RIVER CAVE

By
Jan Eberle Schaberg

Heritage Publishing. US
Bradenton, Florida

CHAPTER ONE

The violent morning storms had finally come to an end. It was hard to believe, with the bright sun and calm wind, that the storms had ever come through.

I have to admit the view from my new tree house was awesome! The mountains looked cooler than ever, but I guess they would from three stories up. Sometimes, I felt like a high society millionaire, looking down from his New York penthouse view at the tiny people walking by.

For the life of me, I couldn't figure out why my grandfather thought it was necessary to build it so high. It was much larger than the original tree house, too. Now, I knew there were plenty of sturdy trees to support it, but I still thought he went a little overboard. Even though Grandpa was retired, he still built a mean tree house!

He built our first club-slash-tree house about four years ago. It was half the size of the new one and only one story up. I guess it was safer for eight-year-olds to hang out in. Now, we're all twelve. With our rock climbing and bouldering experience, I think the folks trusted us to be more careful than most kids. Grandpa didn't cut any corners when it came to the safety of my tree house.

I was just hanging out on the tree house balcony after breakfast when I looked down and noticed my parents sitting in the glass sunroom. It looked like they were drinking tea. They seemed chatty. Mom pointed up at the tree house, and Dad nodded. I wondered what they were up to. There was never a dull moment in the Mandel household. I'm their handsome yet witty son, Dean. Well, maybe not so witty. I have a kid sister named Delilah. Now, she was witty. She did a cute imitation of Joan Rivers, and she's only six years old! Mom was a huge Joan Rivers fan.

Mom's a doctor, and Dad's a full-time U.S. Fire and Aviation Division pilot. It could get exciting around our house. Sometimes, Mom was called away during the night to deliver a baby who just couldn't wait to breathe our fresh Arizona air, and Dad, well, if there was a fire that was out of control, day or night, he was flying. I'm glad us kids had our club.

Our club is called the Young Climbers Club. We all have some or a combination of rock climbing, bouldering, and even expert hiking skills. For all of us, though, caving was a passion. It was mostly for fun. We'd been mentoring kids Delilah's age on low-ground hiking skills, basic survival tips, and reading beginners' maps. It was cool. We always got a charge out of helping little kids.

We'll welcome a new member into the club somewhere down the road. Joining me, Tula, Jonas, and Spooky will be Emma Davis. Until now, there've only been four of us, but with all the mentoring we've been involved in, it would allow each of us more time to participate in our individual competitions. Emma's got a good head on her shoulders and a big heart. In the meantime, I waited for the gang to arrive at my new club-slash-tree house.

I'd been waiting on the balcony all morning. It was the first official day of our Spring Break from school. The four of us decided to take advantage of the great weather by doing a bit of hiking and caving. We were going to warm up at our regular rock-climbing place, followed by an afternoon at Lava River Cave.

We'd originally decided to meet at the newly built tree house first because the gang had been kept away so it wouldn't ruin the big reveal. I was proud of it and my grandfather! It was almost as exciting as a reality show, except we weren't exactly reality star material. Delilah might have fit that bill but was too young and impressionable. Spooky, whose real name is Bartholomew, was the first to arrive. He came up the lift and spotted me on the balcony.

Now, Spooky is a rare character, one you have to appreciate to love. I asked him once why he didn't use his birth name. His answer was predictable yet starkly correct. He just looked at me blankly and replied, "Would *you*?" Yeah, I rest my case.

I was excited when Spooky arrived. He stood at the door with his same silly grin, nodding as he slowly took it all in. I could almost hear his cool theme music, which followed him everywhere.

"Welcome to our new, awesome club-slash-tree house!" I grinned excitedly.

At that moment, we both heard the tonearm of his cool

music scratch across his *serendipitous* moment. That's one of Spooky's favorite words.

"Aw, dude." Spooky shook his head. "Dude, dude, dude. *Why* do you have to go and say something jive like that? You know that jive thing you say? *Club SLASH tree house*? It makes my skin crawl. Peace out, man, and cut out that kid stuff."

"What?" I felt embarrassed and angry. "Okay, smarty, what would you call this place then?" He looked around, scratching his chin as he thought.

"I'd call it The Crib." I just rolled my eyes and shook my head. I couldn't think of any reasonable response.

Just then, I noticed Tula walking across the new balcony. Tula is a totally neat girl. She's a cross between common sense, patience, and far-out imagination, which, by the way, usually pans out. If I had another sister, I'd want it to be Tula. Her parents immigrated from Finland right after high school. I believe they came to the United States as exchange students and then returned to complete their studies. They're a real success story and have become American citizens. Her mother is a foreign interpreter in seven languages, and her dad is an archaeologist.

I'd never seen any other person Tula's age with gray hair and ice-blue eyes. She joined the club when she was eight. That's when I said something about her gray hair, which I thought was neat. I remember she replied coolly, "It's ash-blonde, not gray." That was followed up by a grin and a wink.

I peeked out to greet her. "Well, cuz, what do you think?" She stretched out her arms and spun in a circle. She looked like Julie Andrews in her famous spinning scene on the mountain from The Sound of Music. We watch it every year with Nana.

She loves that scene.

"I must give Gramps a big hug! He's brilliant! This is perfect." She snooped into the cupboards Grandpa built, where we stored the cushions for the wooden benches. We always kept a first-aid kit in the first tree house and had a new, suped-up version donated by Mom. There was also a nice cooler for those long meetings or occasional lunches.

"I'm glad you like it, Tula." I thought I'd take the opportunity for our first official vote by suggesting ideas for the best name to call our club-slash-tree house. "Hey, Tula, Spook and I were talking earlier about what to call this new venture. He likes The Crib. What are your thoughts?"

"Hmm, let me think about that for a while." Tula continued to investigate every nook and cranny. She seemed fascinated.

As if on cue, Jonas rounded the corner and stood at the doorway, looking around in that 'Jonas' kind of way. Jonas is, well, in a word, a sap, but in a good way. When he looked at someone or something, it was as if he were gazing into the core of the Milky Way in total wonderment. He looked at a hotdog the same way he looked at a rainbow. Jonas also possessed this uncanny need to turn on the weepy faucet. Honest to Pete, he could cry at the drop of a hat.

It is an emotional cry, not necessarily a sad cry. We nicknamed him our official mush-ball.

There was one particular item about his father that awe-inspired each of us. Mr. Falk had accompanied an elite group of snow climbers for an incredibly challenging expedition on Mount Everest. He was one of the few to have completed this dangerous effort. His Mom is an awesome teacher. It's no wonder Jonas is well-spoken at our age.

"Jonas, my man!" We high-fived. "So, did Grandpa capture the essence of OZ?" Of course, I was being totally sarcastic, which he'd come to expect from his fellow club members. He turned and looked at me but didn't utter a word. He just stared at me as his eyes began to well with tears. Aw, geez. "So, I take it you like it?" I exclaimed.

"This is truly a tribute to Mr. Mandel's keen and detailed capabilities. I'm inspired." A few tears trickled down his cheeks.

"Well," Tula chimed in suddenly, "I think I have my name suggestion." Jonas spun around as if regaining his composure.

"What are you all talking about?" I explained what we were doing, and Jonas didn't need more than a second for his answer. The three of us waited on bated breath.

"The Crystalline Cloud. *Ahhh.*" He grinned into space as if he was having an out-of-body experience. Spooky glanced over the rim of his glasses. Tula also remained silent, biting her lower lip, and I rolled my eyes again.

"Tula, what was your thought?" I knew it couldn't possibly be as horrible as the other two nincompoops. She grinned sensibly into the room.

"How about Home Base?" I told you! Her sensibility and imagination always meet at just the right place! It was perfect.

"Tula, you have my vote." I glanced at Spooky. "Spook? Jonas? What say you?"

They both gave their most enthusiastic thumbs up. Thank goodness that was over. Now, we could focus our day on fun.

CHAPTER TWO

After finishing our lunch, the gang and I piled into Mom's SUV and headed to one of our regular rock-climbing gyms. There were three or four we liked best because they had the most challenging climbs and the best instructors. We learned most of what we learned over the past several years from them. They were experienced; we knew we could count on them to prepare us for a competition.

As it turned out, all of us were participating in upcoming competitions and enjoyed tightening skills together. We'd decided it would benefit our core balance and flexibility to head to nearby Lava River Cave. The three-quarter mile cave was a challenge, one we looked forward to every time we went. After a few hours of shopping, Mom picked us up and dropped us at the cave. Tula's Dad agreed to pick us up a few hours later.

I remember the first time I saw Lava River Cave. Now, I grew up in Arizona. My parents moved from Phoenix to Flagstaff when I was five years old. Undoubtedly, I've seen a lot of cool, natural stuff, like caves, crevasses, and, of course, the Grand Canyon. Lava River Cave was right up there on my top cool list. It's called a tube cave, the longest in Arizona. Grandpa told me the cave was discovered by a lumberman back in the early 1900's.

Tula's Dad, the archaeologist, said the cave was formed about 700,000 years ago by molten rock that erupted from a volcanic vent. My brain can't imagine 700,000 years. Anyhow, first, the top, bottom, and sides cooled and solidified. After that, the insides of the lava river kept flowing, emptying the cave into what we see today. Serendipitous, as Spooky would say.

There are small, wavy ripples on the floor and super *rad* icicles hanging from the ceiling! In the summer, the inside of the cave can be as cold as forty-five degrees. The rocks are always sharp and slippery. We've each had our share of injuries, but nothing serious. I always remind the gang to bring extra light sources because if one fails, traveling before the next light source can be a long, dark mile.

For some reason, I can't remember. The gang decided to get out of Mr. Van Hanen's car on the back side of the cave. We almost never did this, but I guess an extra mile of hiking to the cave opening wouldn't have hurt. That's when Jonas first saw the dancing leaves.

"Hey Jonas, what are you staring at?" He looked like he was in some kind of trance. He was staring at the back side of the cave, which was basically just rock and dirt with a few bushes growing wild. He slowly raised his hand and pointed at the cave.

"Do you see that?" he whispered. I wasn't sure what he was looking at.

"See what? What are you looking at?" I whispered back.

"Those leaves. See? Over the cave. They're dancing around on a wave of wind." I continued to look. "Do you see it now?" He pointed my head to where he was looking.

"Oh, yeah, that's cool, Jonas. What do you make of it? I mean, what does it mean?" I was stumped. Wind, blowing leaves?

"I think there's a wind source coming from the cave. A crack, a hole, or some way that the cave seems to be expelling the wind." He looked over at me and continued to whisper. "The cave is lavatized across the entire length with no breaches. Supposedly, it's been like that for 700,000 some -odd years."

"Jonas, I don't think lavatized is a word, but I know what you mean. That's some strong draft. It's a lot of wind coming through a tiny hole." I thought for a moment about the cave's history, which we all knew pretty well. "According to all the literature about the cave, there are no hollow areas where wind would possibly come from. It's as solid as hardened lava gets." We looked at each other, mouths opened. Spooky snuck up behind us.

"Hey, you two. What are we whispering about?" We explained what we'd seen. "Well, you know that National Geological Center took ex-ray type film years ago, and Dean's right. It's as solid as it gets. Lava River Cave ends here. Period. That's what they claim."

Before I knew it, Tula joined in. "I studied the Earth's mantle in depth this past fall for a book report and found that the mantle's *so-called* transition zone is capable of masking or hiding underground water beneath it. Is it possible it can also hide large pockets of air or spaces that may have been dug out, for instance?" That piece of information caught our attention.

"Tula, don't you think that's a little deep into the earth? I mean, you're talking miles below.

We think it could be maybe feet or yards below." I watched her mind work for a moment.

"Maybe so, but who said a man-made breach wasn't created somehow that was never seen by geological film?" Her icy blue eyes began to sparkle as we all looked at her in amazement.

"Tula, you're a genius!" Jonas couldn't resist his boyish wonderment.

"Shh!" We didn't want Jonas to get any unnecessary attention. At this point, our suspicions were top secret. Spooky pulled one of his serendipitous ideas out of thin air.

"Dudes, who has a couple of spare shoelaces?" We all rummaged through our backpacks.

"I do!" Tula squealed. "A pair, but they're pink. Sorry."

"No," said Spooky with excitement, "they're perfect. Jonas, take me to the wind pocket."

The two walked over and, as discreetly as they could, tied the laces and dropped them into the tiny opening. I thought their idea was good. Thin, but good. Frankly, I didn't think anything fantastic would come of all this. I urged everyone to start hiking because we were wasting precious daylight.

We arrived at the cave's entrance about fifteen minutes later. We wasted more time than I thought because the cave keeper gave everyone the final hours' notice before closing. As usual, we flew through pretty quickly. No one managed to slip on any ice patches, which was good because our competitions were all coming up that week. We didn't pass anyone going in, so we assumed we were the last. This allowed us to snoop around for the infamous pink shoelaces.

I thought it would be a good idea if someone stood guard at the entrance, so I sent Jonas with one of our two walkie-talkies. There is no satellite, texting, or cell phone service. The only good a cell phone did was for the flashlight device and camera. There was not much to photograph in the dark.

Tula, Spooky, and I snooped around in the near dark for a while. I checked in on Jonas every five minutes to see if anyone entered the cave. There was no one else. I decided I would get up against where the floor and the cave wall met, which was extremely tight. Spooky was too big, and I didn't want Tula banging herself up. This was literally the tightest part of the cave, and I felt uncomfortable, almost phobic. I was feeling short of breath. I reached my hand behind a small rock, just in front of where the cave dead-ended. Suddenly, I felt something hard and cold, like iron or steel. It felt like a lever or handle of some kind. I quickly yanked my hand out.

"Holy cow, what the heck was that?" I exclaimed. Their eyes grew large with surprise.

"What did it feel like, dude? Was it alive?" Spooky seemed uneasy.

"I'm not sure. It felt like something metal, steel, or iron. Sort of like a lever or handle of some sort." They looked at each other, their faces a bit pale.

"Well," urged Tula, "which did it feel like? A lever or a handle? Hey, I know. I use my pin flash and cell phone camera. See if you can get a shot of it."

"I can try." I knew it would be a stretch because I couldn't move much at all, jammed inside the floor crevice. "There."

I handed the phone back to Tula. "I think I got a picture of something or maybe just dirt." Tula and Spooky stared at the cell phone screen for a minute.

"Dude, I see something, but I'm not quite sure what." Spooky was his usual big help. Tula asked if I was pushing or pulling it.

"Yes, I'm doing both, and it didn't budge. It may never budge, and it may be absolutely nothing. I think we're getting all jazzed up for no reason." Just then, Tula gently moved me aside.

"Do you mind if I try? We've come all this way, and it wouldn't hurt to try one more time. We'll probably be heading out in a few minutes anyway."

"Sure, why not?" She lay on the dirt floor where I had been.

"What does it feel like to you?" I asked her curiously.

"Hmm, well, it feels like a release lever of some kind. Dang, it's cold to touch! Can you hand me one of my gloves, please?" She continued to fiddle with it, but she wasn't successful. "Hey, hold on a minute. Let me try twisting the stupid thing instead."

All at once, the rock wall right in front of us shook gently, then moved up right into the ceiling of the cave, but how? The three of us just stood there, shaking. I recall saying a few choice words I usually don't say. Geez, if my father heard me, he'd ground me.

"What in holy blazes do you make of this? It looks like an opening into a large room, but how? How, when the cave ended here?" We stood quietly. Spooky was the first to step in. His hair blew around from the wind, the same wind we felt behind the back of the cave earlier. He stopped and took a deep breath. "Spook, be careful. Here, take my flashlight."

"Dean, should I talkie Jonas to come in or stay down?" I stood staring in shock. "Deano?"

"I'll do it. Spot Spook, would you?" I hit the talkie button for Jonas. "Hey, cuz, what do you see? C'mon back."

"Well, nothing and no one," he whispered, " I've been watching for the cave guard. I think he went toward the gate area. Can I come down? Come back."

"Yeah, but be careful. It's dark now. Hey, Jonas? We found something. Come back."

"Oh yeah? Do you mean like pink shoelaces? Come back." He sounded hopeful.

"Not exactly. It's bigger than a breadbox. See you in about fifteen minutes and, cuz, be careful. Out."

By then, Tula had also stepped into the mysterious room. I felt uneasy because I didn't know if the door would close and lock them inside. Spooky shined the big flashlight slowly, sweeping the room starting on the floor. We laughed when we spotted the infamous pink shoelaces several feet away. It verified our suspicions and that some sort of room was added later than the time of the cave's discovery in 1915.

"Spooky, shine straight ahead at your ten o'clock. What's that?" His flashlight shined on a small oak barrel used as a makeshift table. An oil lamp sat on top of it. We were shocked by our discovery. "Well, I'll go to heck, you guys! We might be able to get some light in here. Does anyone know if oil goes bad?"

"Nah, I don't think so, dude. It won't work if it's too dirty or damp. Here, I've got my Bic with me." Spooky gave me his lighter, and I gingerly walked toward the makeshift table. "Hey, somebody has to stay outside the door in case it closes,"

I spoke too soon.

"Uh-oh," said Tula calmly. "It should be okay. The door should be on some sort of primitive sensor, even if it's only weight-bearing. Here, watch as I step toward the threshold." She confidently moved toward the door. She was right. The door opened the moment she reached it. There is no doubt something else she learned in science class. I just rolled my eyes. Again. As if on cue, Jonas stood staring with wonderment at our discovery.

"Oh, bloody heck! Am I dreaming? Hey, did you find the pink shoelaces?" Spooky held them over his head as he fiddled with the mantle in the oil lamp. "Do you want some help, Spooky?" "Yeah. Hey, Jonas, if you would wet the wick down into the oil for a minute and crank it back up, I'll try to light the bugger." After a few minutes, a golden light illuminated the rock walls. We could see each other for the first time since we were outside a few hours earlier. Boy, the gang was a sight for sore eyes, all in smiles. I glanced at Jonas, who was looking sort of 'pasty.' He fainted!

"Jonas! Jonas!" Tula ran to him right away. "He seems to have just passed out. Thank goodness his head landed on my backpack." She smiled. "I'll sit with him. He'll come to in a minute."

"Spook! Tula! Do you see what I see?" We stood with our eyes fixed, unable to move. I walked slowly over to what appeared to be a picture. "I can't read the bottom. It's got a little dirt on it." I strained my eyes a bit. "Vinc. Vinc? Does that make any sense to you guys?"

"Vinc?" Spooky looked puzzled. "I wonder if that's the name of the picture, maybe the place in the picture? Hmm,

Vinc." In our silence, Jonas sat up and looked at Vinc.

"For my part, I know nothing with any certainty, but seeing the stars makes me dream." We turned and stared at Jonas, who was smiling tearfully. "It's not a picture, it's a painting, and it's not called Vinc. It's titled, 'The Painter on his Way to Work'." He walked softly toward the painting and crouched on one knee, gently blowing dirt from the bottom. "The artist," He paused for a moment. "Is Vincent Van Gogh. With dirt, Vincent looked like Vinc. He only ever signed his first name." Jonas stood and walked over to us. "And, what I recited was one of his famous quotes." We were all stunned by Jonas' knowledge of art and artists.

"Jonas, where did you learn all this stuff about art?" I was more than curious.

"Well, my mother minored in art classics in college. It's her first love, but she decided to teach elementary school instead." He smiled as he talked about his mom. "When I was much younger, like six or seven, Mom and I would sit at the kitchen table for hours looking through her art books. She stopped to tell me stories about each one of them. Van Gogh is just one of many. It is pretty cool, you know?" I smiled at the gift his mom shared with him.

That was the day that changed everything for the members of the Young Climbers Club. What were we doing? What were we going to do? We asked ourselves and each other that question as we stood in the cave, lit brightly by an old oil lamp. We sat on the floor in front of the painting for a while and took in every brush stroke. We'd never been in the presence of genuine, honest-to-goodness art. It was awesome.

I knew it was time to call Grandpa.

CHAPTER THREE

By then, I had a lot of questions rolling around in my head, like, where did the painting come from? How did it get there? Who put it there and why? I knew the gang needed help. I immediately thought of my grandfather and father.

By then I had a Grandpa's name is Theodore, but Nana Sarah called him Teddy. He'd always been an ultra-patriot who said he was bound for any great cause. After graduating from high school, Grandpa joined the Army and served four years in the Vietnam War. When he got home in 1972, he started college and studied Forestry. During his off time, he became a member of the local fire department, and it became his passion.

He found himself a member of the U.S. Forestry and Aviation, just like Dad had years later, except Grandpa didn't fly planes. He became an elite member of the famed Hotshot Crew and helped control some of the worst fires in the history of the Grand Canyon fires. The name Hotshot references the hottest part of the fire. Eventually, he became a boss over the crews.

Dad's story was a little different. He joined the army in 1998 for four years after college at the age of twenty-two. Dad studied Aerospace Engineering. He'd also gotten his pilot's license and was considered a master pilot. So, when he joined the Army, he earned a place in the 160th Special Operations Aviation Regiment (Airborne). That's a long name for an elite group of flyers. They're nicknamed Night Stalkers.

Some years later, after 911, Dad was called back in 2011 to become part of a special operation led by the CIA. It was called Operation Neptune Spear. This was a special operation to be a part of. It was the plan that ended the life of the infamous terrorist leader, Usama bin Laden.

I was only seven years old then, and I remember being scared when he left. Delilah was a baby. My mom was brave for all of us. She kept us happy and calm during those months when Dad was overseas. The day he came home was one of my favorite days ever!

Okay, so I thought back to Grandpa. After he retired, he and Nana began making changes to the ranch. They converted one of the huge barns into temporary housing with nice beds, showers, and washing facilities. Oh, and did I mention cable television? He put an extension off the kitchen so Nana could fit two large tables for big meals. Who, you ask, would be eating, sleeping, and watching cable TV? None other than Hotshot Crews!

Many of the crew members came from other parts of the country. Their seasonal shift time could last for weeks or months. The heart of the season runs from May till September, but many were permanent members like Grandpa had been. He was retired, and this was his new gig.

I trusted my grandfather almost more than anyone. I needed to tell someone what had happened to us in the cave.

The gang and I found a Van Gogh painting in Lava River Cave.

When I said those words out loud, they were unbelievable to me.

CHAPTER FOUR

As soon as the gang and I reached the cave entrance, we called Grandpa on my cell phone. I suspected he wouldn't be happy because it was 10:30 at night! Thank goodness his ranch wasn't that far from the cave. After I was able to calm him down, I explained why I was calling, and he listened quietly.

"I know it's late for us to be out, Grand, but this favor is more important than anything I ever asked you for before."

"Well, I know you have a good head on your shoulders, Dean. I trust you. First, are you all okay?" I turned and gave a thumbs-up to the gang, who seemed relieved.

"Absolutely fine. So, here's the thing. We just came out of the cave." I hesitated for a minute as I blurted it all out. "With a Van Gogh painting. We found a secret lever under the rocks at the very end of the cave and found ourselves inside the cave. Then, we found an oil lamp sitting on this makeshift table. Spooky lit it, Jonas fainted, and Tula turned out to be a whiz at counterweight rock doors, which opened when she walked on it." The phone was silent for a minute.

I could hear Grandpa breathing. "Grandpa?"

"I'm here. Leaving out all the other wild antics till later, how do you know it's a Van Gogh painting?"

"Jonas identified it. It's, well, it's beautiful, Grandpa. I've never, ever seen anything like it!"

"Ah yes, of course. Jonas' mother is an art expert. Her stories certainly made an impression on Jonas." He paused for a moment. "Did you leave the painting in the cave, or did you manage to get it out unharmed?"

"It's with us, and it's perfect. We need you, Grandpa. The night security is up at the gate now. If we use the shortcut to the road and bypass the gate, can we meet you there somewhere?" I was nervous because I knew this was a lot to ask of Grandpa and Nana.

"You know, your folks will be worried out of their mind over you?" Nana Sarah came on the phone. She seemed worried about us, but I think she knew we were about as responsible as twelve gets.

"I know, Nana. I told a fib. I'm sorry for this, but I told them the gang, and I were having sleepovers at your new digs. I guess they probably think we're already tucked in bed by now." The phone was silent.

"Let's not make a habit of this, Dean. Your folks trust you and can handle the truth. They're cool, remember?"

"You're the greatest, Nana. I promise I'll call them first thing in the morning and apologize for lying to them. It might be a good idea to get through tonight first."

"Grandpa is on his way. He said to hide behind the old Wrigley Chewing Gum billboard. He'll stop and get you there."

I was relieved and eager to get to the ranch. We were dirty and hungrier than I've ever been. Knowing Nana, food would be waiting for us when we got there.

We made it safely to the billboard and hid behind it so that no passing drivers would see a group of twelve-year-olds holding a Van Gogh painting. Funny, I know, but true. We jumped into Grandpa's SUV carefully with the painting. He turned on the inside cabin lights and spun around to see the painting. His eyes grew large as he stared at it for a moment.

"Yep, that's a Van Gogh." He stopped for a minute and laughed as he shook his head. "This is crazy! Crazier than anything I've been up against. Nana will freak out!" We all started to laugh.

After the twenty-minute drive to the ranch, Nana met us on the front driveway. The smell of freshly grilled hamburgers poured out through the front door. She stopped dead in her tracks and stared at the painting. She placed her hand over her mouth and shook her head.

"It's true. It's true. 'The Painter on his Way to Work.' She looked over at us. "It's one of Van Gogh's self-portraits, isn't it, Jonas." They smiled at each other as Jonas walked up to hug Nana.

"Yes, Nana Mandel, it is, and it's a beauty." Tears welled in his eyes, mush-ball strikes again.

We all went inside, cleaned up, and dove head-first into the delicious food. After we ate, Grandpa, who had been pretty quiet, sat us down in the living room.

"Grandpa," I asked, hoping for an answer, "What do you make of all this?"

"I can't say for sure, Dean-o. A few things come to mind

that sound a bit too far-fetched at the moment. Yet, nothing else makes any sense. I want you all to fill me in with as many details as you can recall of the cave room you discovered, how it works, and what else was in the room. This might help me formulate a better scenario than the wacky one I have right now."

We talked to Nana and Grandpa for a while until we couldn't keep our eyes open. Nana ushered us to the guest rooms, boys in one and Tula in the other. I'm sure we all snoozed out soon after we hit the bed. I laid there for a few minutes thinking about how lucky I was to have grandparents like these. I prayed that night for safety, protection, faith, and guidance, and please God, watch over us.

I slept like a log that night. The clock on the nightstand read 9:30. I sat up quickly and rubbed my eyes before taking another look at the clock. It didn't lie. Fortunately, I was overcome by the smell of bacon! One of my favorite food groups. I looked over at the two twin beds, and the guys were still asleep. I figure if they didn't wake up in time, they might forfeit their share of bacon.

After all, it would be rude to wake them up.

I heard giggling coming from the kitchen. I washed my face and ran down the hall toward the amazing smell of bacon. Tula and Nana were talking and snickering when I arrived in the kitchen. The table was set. Tula had already squeezed fresh juice and was getting ready to toast the fresh bread. Nana had a dozen eggs in a bowl ready for the flattop.

"Morning, sleepy head. Did you rest well?" Nana said in her usual chipper voice.

"Yes, very well. I don't remember anything after I shut my eyes." I looked over to see Tula folding the napkins near the plates. "How long have you been up?" I was curious.

"Oh, since dawn. I went for a ten-mile jog, milked the cows, snagged eggs from the chickens, you know, typical chores." She winked as usual.

"Wait a minute, there are no cows or chickens here." The girls busted out laughing. "Oh, you two. Say, where is the bacon? If you and Grandpa ever get anything besides horses for the ranch, pigs would be my vote. Bacon for all!" Sometimes, I crack myself up.

"Ewe!" squealed Tula. "That's gross, Dean Mandel. Just gross," she said as she took a hardy bite of bacon with a smirk. I smirked back. I heard Grandpa on the phone in the den down the hall. I heard him say, David. That's my dad's name. I gulped hard. Grandpa walked into the room.

"Hey, morning, you two. I hope you're hungry because Nana cooked enough for a hungry Hotshots Crew!" We all laughed at the piles of food. Little did I know then the food would disappear in a matter of minutes. I pulled Grandpa aside.

"Hey, 'grand, not to eavesdrop, but was that my Dad you were talking to?" I gulped hard again.

"Yes, as a matter of fact."

"Well, was he mad? I mean, I haven't had the time this morning to apologize to him yet."

"No, not really. A bit surprised. There was a lot to take in because I told him what I knew so far. You'll have a chance to have a heart-to-heart with him later. It's all good." He smiled. "We spent almost an hour on the phone discussing ideas and possibilities, among other things. We agreed on three things so far: going back to the cave, bringing the other parents into this, and telling no one. Absolutely, positively no one until we get a handle on this and the ramifications involved."

"Like what?" I didn't understand what he was talking about.

"Well, the possibility that the art might be stolen. It certainly belonged to someone, whether or not the person or persons who put it in the cave were the owners. Our best chance at concluding something workable is if we, you kids and us parents, talk together and discuss what should be done."

"Grandpa, would you and Nana be willing to hide the art for the time being? You have lots of secret places, more than we do." I was hoping he would agree.

"It's already done. I'll take you to it after breakfast. Meantime, the last one to the pile of bacon does the dishes!" As if drawn by the smell of breakfast, Jonas and Spooky sat at the table. Grandpa said grace for us and took a moment to reassure us. "Listen, today is going to be a trying, stressful day. Many of our questions may go unanswered. If we keep an open mind and stay on course, with a little prayer, we may know what needs to be done. Agreed?" We all nodded.

"Dig in!" Nana declared.

As always, when Nana cooked, Grandpa did the dishes. One time, he said that their arrangement had worked out well for all the years they were married, and he wasn't about to fix it now—sound advice.

CHAPTER FIVE

Nana decided to drive us home after breakfast before running errands. She dropped me off at home last. We chatted for a minute before Nana squeezed me tight and reassured me that everything would work out. She told me she was proud of me, but I asked her why. She answered that she was proud of me for being me. Geez, grown-ups.

When I walked in, Delilah came running in and gave me one of her powerhouse hugs! Mom followed her. I think everyone was glad we were okay. It didn't hit me until then what had actually happened the night before. It was a big deal, I guess.

I went into the den where Dad was waiting for me. He didn't scold me. I was relieved and told him so. He smiled and told me he understood completely. He also said he didn't know if he would've had the guts to be as levelheaded as we were. He was proud, but I didn't get off completely without a warning and the importance of being truthful. I got the message loud and clear. He was right.

I took a much-needed shower and let the hot water beat on me for a while so I could think. Grandpa had arranged a meeting at our house that afternoon. He invited the other parents to join us. It would, no doubt, be a big powwow, a chance to throw out as many ideas as we could come up with. So far, all I knew was that Dad and Grandpa wanted to go with us to revisit the cave. Our plan was a repeat of the first time when we stowed away after the park closed. It wasn't an idea the grown-ups were jazzed about, but no one else had one any better.

The most important thing so far was for all of us to stay quiet about the painting, the cave, and anything else connected to last night. Surprisingly, The gang was on board, and so were the folks. I was proud that they could look at this as an adventure. Somehow, I was sure it would be. I didn't understand how much.

Later that afternoon, everyone arrived for the meeting. Jonas with Mr. & Mrs. Falk, Tula with Mr. & Mrs. Van Hanen, and Spooky with Senator & Mrs. Jordan. Spooky's Dad was a Senator in Arizona. My grandparents arrived last. We gathered in the den while Grandpa picked up some notes he'd made and started our meeting.

"Thank you all for coming on such short notice. Sometimes some things just can't wait, I'm sure you'll agree. By now, you all know the basics and have had a short time to think about possible ideas that will lead to a resolution. I made a few notes I'd like to share with you but wanted to know if anyone had questions first." Senator Jordan raised his hand.

"I know that all four kids have competitions before the end of the week. Would you suggest going back to the cave before then? I know how hard they all work to prepare for these events." Grandpa nodded.

"Once we find out when the events will be, we can formulate an idea. Let's see, today is Tuesday. Show of hands, who has a competition before Friday? No one? Great. This means, Senator, that we can likely return to the cave tomorrow night if that's all right with everyone else?" Spooky's dad nodded in agreement.

"That works for me, and please, just call me Bill." Everyone else seemed to agree so far.

Grandpa began reading some of his notes.

"I don't know if this is just my practical side talking, but I feel the first order of business, after revisiting the cave for pictures and notes, is to authenticate the painting. I'm sure we all agree that we're reasonably savvy when looking at fine art. It's unlikely that any of us can truly authenticate the piece, agreed?" Everyone nodded. "I served in the Army and have been lifelong friends with an art dealer from Chicago who, in his field, is quite well known and thought of. Would there be any objection to his authenticating the art?"

"Would he be willing to travel to Arizona?" Tula's Mom raised her hand. "I wouldn't think shipping the art would be wise, considering the possibility it could be stolen."

"I would agree, Elsa. I'm confident he would be intrigued to be part of this project. He'll likely bring an assistant and a few tools of the trade. Now, if he should find that the art is fake, I recommend we contact the authorities and put it into their hands. We don't want to be involved with any potential stolen art rings!" Everyone laughed and mumbled a few words to the person next to them. Dad raised his hand. "David?"

"It might be helpful if my father, the kids, and I get together after our cave visit tomorrow night to put down as many notes as possible from the visit. I also agree that photographs will be helpful." He paused for a moment and continued. "Would everyone be available to meet again, say, Sunday afternoon? The competitions will be over, and the notes and photos will be organized and available. Show of hands? Okay, that's all of you, great!" I stood to be recognized.

"Grandpa, what happens if the painting is authentic?" I was curious to hear his answer.

"Well, Dean, I think at that point, if Ernie Heinz, the art dealer, declares it to be authentic, he will probably have a protocol he would follow. One important thought to keep in mind is that we're all in agreement with every step we take. We have a lot to lose if we don't. No one needs to feel uncomfortable." The gang and their folks all pretty much answered together. It was unanimous that we wanted to see this exciting adventure through.

The following day was filled with preparation for our second visit to Lava River Cave since discovering the art inside the secret room. The gang and I were excited, but the parents seemed stressed out. I suppose the idea that we'd be breaking the park rules again didn't set well, but we had no choice. We had to be all in. For the gang, it was no skin off our nose. I think we were also proud to show off our discovery. No words we'd used to describe it to that point would trump the real deal. Seeing was believing.

Dad, Grandpa, Nana Sarah, and the gang piled into Grandpa's SUV. We'd packed our backpacks with the usual stuff for caving: gloves, two or three light sources, a few bandages, water, and a knit cap to keep our heads warm. It could be cold in the cave, especially because we planned to be there much longer. My father brought his digital camera, a tape measure, and plenty of paper and pencils.

CHAPTER SIX

The main gist of the plan was that Nana was our driver. She agreed to park discreetly behind the Wrigley's Gum bill-board and wait the two hours, or so we would need to complete our task. We were all familiar with the cave, which included Grandpa and Nana. They'd run through it many times and were maybe even more familiar than the gang. So, as planned, she dropped us off shortly before the security guard would call at the last entrance to Lava Cave. We put on our best tourist behavior.

Just as it had been two days before, we passed practically no one on the way in. Jonas agreed to be our outside walkie-talkie communication again. It worked out well because he was scared to go back into the secret room.

We arrived after an uneventful trip into the cave and set our sacks on the ground. Tula hit the floor and reached her gloved hand into the rock bed. After a minute, she located and twisted the iron lever, which automatically opened the cave door. The look on Grandpa's face was priceless. It was well worth the price of admission! The door opened as expected with a rumble as the door disappeared into the ceiling of the cave. We shined several flashlights into the room as Spooky lit the oil lamp with his trusty Bic lighter. We all grinned at the success of our mission so far.

Just then, we heard an unexpected noise coming down the cave.

"Quick, everyone into the cave so we can close the door!" I whispered to everyone as I pushed them all in quickly. Just as before, the door closed behind us. "Is everyone in here?" I got responses from each member of our team. "Okay, let's be quiet and listen for a minute." We stood motionless for five minutes, which felt more like five hours. Finally, we heard a woman's voice. "Oh geez, is that Nana?"

"Hullo? Hey, troops, are you here?" I moved toward the door to trigger its opening. "Well," Nana exclaimed, "Isn't this just like a James Bond movie? Ooh-wee! Is this cool, or what?"

"Nana!" I exclaimed. "What are you doing here? Are you alright? Where's the car?" I was frantic that she'd hurt herself.

"Well, the car is where I left it. I'm fine, sonny-boy, and I'm here because it turns out I wasn't a very good listener." She and Grandpa laughed and winked at each other. "So, let me in, and let's get on with it."

We spent about an hour in the cave, taking pictures and measurements and picking up anything we found, even if it was something stupid. Grandpa always said no question was stupid, and no stone should ever be unturned. Our second trip to the secret room was a treat to me and the gang because we saw many things we didn't see the first time. For instance, one was some scribble on the wall that we couldn't make out well. Dad took pictures of it to be analyzed.

Another was an old cigarette pack and some butts nearby. We kept it all.

After some much-needed time of taking in this remarkable hour inside our newfound cave, we reluctantly left. It wouldn't be the last time.

CHAPTER SEVEN

That night, we left the cave with an idea of what might have happened many years earlier. We knew someone had planned the storage room in the cave and purposely put the painting there.

There were also signs that more than one person was there. We found some trash that hadn't totally disintegrated. We found two brands of cigarette butts. There was also a brown paper bag crumpled into a ball with writing on it we couldn't read. Next, we picked up some brown paper with writing on it that we knew wasn't English.

All these things would be kept in a cool, dry place until Grandpa's friend, the art dealer, arrived. Mostly, we were tired from the hike in and out of the cave a second night. My mom had my equipment and backpack packed and ready. She was driving me to the competition in my hometown of Phoenix. I was excited about this competition because it was my first involvement in the new age class. I was competing against thirteen- and fourteen-year-olds who were a little stronger and more experienced than I. My strength was my agility, thanks to daily yoga. Mom and I sometimes did yoga together in the morning before school unless I ran late.

I looked forward to the competition and considered it a much-needed distraction. Those past few days had been like a dream but heavy. In the meantime, Dad and Grandpa were taking each item, photographing it, and documenting each of them in a sort of diary.

So far, half of us thought the art was stolen, and half of us felt a person or people hid it in the cave to keep others from getting it. Besides that, we were clueless.

It wasn't enough that the gang, our parents, and grandparents knew about the hidden cave room and the beautiful art.

Somehow, I still felt the need to tell everyone I knew! You know when you have a secret, and the more you're told *not* to tell, the more you *need* to tell? Well, it was sort of like that. I knew I had to keep my big boy pants on, though, now more than ever. I admit I felt much better after whispering our secret to my dog, Bo. His wagging tail said it all.

The drive to Phoenix was a little over two hours. By the end of the day, I was worn out and just plain tired from the night before. However, I managed to take second place in a competition field of about twenty-eight. I was shocked, shocked and pleased. Mom said she was knocked over by a feather. I think that's good. I ended up sleeping all the way home. I scarcely remember crawling into bed.

CHAPTER EIGHT

Saturday morning was bright and sunny. After breakfast, I had the chance to wander into the den to see what Dad and Grandpa had done with the samples we brought back from the cave Thursday night.

My father was meticulous about almost everything. Staging our cave items was no different. He took some corkboard and straight pins and fastened all the items, even the cigarette butts, to it. Next to each item was a photo of where in the cave it was found. He also pinned a small index card next to it with a description of the item.

Dad told me Grandpa finally went home at ten o'clock Friday night. Knowing Grandpa, he probably spent even more time in his study, contemplating the meaning of it all. Whatever "it" was. We weren't sure. A heist? A secret hiding place? One thing was for sure: we would learn answers to some of those questions through the art dealer's authentication. Saturday morning, after I ate breakfast with Grandpa, he made a cell phone call to his friend, Ernie Heinz.

"Good morning, Heinz Midtown Gallery. How may I assist you?" A pleasant, welcoming voice greeted Grandpa Saturday morning.

"Good morning, my name is Theodore Mandel. May I please speak to Ernie Heinz?" He was excited to talk to his old friend.

"May I tell him what your inquiry is in reference to?" the woman asked.

"Well, could you just mention it's 'Rosie,' please?" Grandpa grinned from ear to ear.

"Certainly. One moment, please." He was only on hold for a minute or so when he heard the familiar voice of his old friend.

"Rosie! Rosie! How the heck are you? How's the family? And lovely Sarah?" Ernie Heinz was a chuckling sort of guy.

"Oh, we're all just fine, Ernie. My golf game hasn't improved any, but besides that, can't complain." Grandpa took a minute to collect his thoughts. "Ernie, remember when we were in the trench in Viet Nam, the night the Viet Cong slammed our troop? After you and I survived that, we spent the night under some brush. Remember we promised that if either of us was in real need of help, we could depend on the other?" The phone was silent for a moment.

"Geez, Rosie, you're scaring me. Is everything all right?" Grandpa didn't answer right away.

"Ted? Talk to me. We're on secure land lines."

"Well," said Grandpa, "I'll save the minute details until later, but it's like this: I'm in possession of something I'm not supposed to have." He sighed loudly. "Okay, Dean and his club found an uncharted room under Lava River Cave. They found a painting inside the room that seriously represents itself as a Van Gogh. We took it out, didn't tell anyone, went back to the secret room, and found some other things, just tidbits of evidence, that contain notes in what looks to be German." He swallowed hard. "Do you know where I'm going with this, Ernie?"

"Holy smokes, Rosie. You've got yourself in a real pickle here." Ernie paused for a second. "I can grab an assistant and a pilot for the jet tonight. I'll bring whatever I might need to identify this painting. By the way, does anyone know which Van Gogh It's supposed to be if it were real?" He was anxious to know.

"'The Painter on His Way to Work'. Why do you ask?" Grandpa was curious.

"Oh my! I'm not sure how to tell you this, but this is either a fake or a miracle."

"Ernie, what do you mean, a miracle?"

"Rosie, this Van Gogh was documented to have been hanging in the Kaiser-Friedrich Museum in Germany when the United States bombed Germany in World War II. It's documented to have been destroyed." Grandpa didn't know what to say. He was shocked.

"What does this mean if you authenticate the painting?"

"It means, Rosie, that we'd have to find an heir deserving of the art. This could get exciting, my boy. Just like old times, Ted! Strap yourself in for a ride! I'll see you about eight o'clock this evening." They both laughed like kids and couldn't control themselves from the excitement. Geez, grown-ups.

After hanging up, Grandpa told the rest of his talk with Mr. Heinz. We were shocked! We were also scared. It became clear that this whole deal was about more than the painting. The question of stolen art was now real. It was obvious that our club desperately needed the help of grown-up professionals. We could never have handled this on our own, although Grandpa insisted we were handling all the excitement very well. Not according to the butterflies in my stomach.

Grandpa wanted to leave some of the details for Ernie Heinz to explain. His knowledge and experience were important to us—and the fact that he was taking a chance with us and this mess. I think Mr. Heinz was partly involved because he couldn't resist the challenge. Spooky thinks Mr. Heinz wanted to help us because of his tight friendship and time in Vietnam with Rosie. Yes, and by the way, we asked Grandpa where on earth he got a nickname like Rosie.

It was pretty simple, in a grown-up sort of way. Grandpa's first name was Theodore or Teddy to his family and friends. Apparently, Mr. Heinz thought he had a stately profile like President Theodore Roosevelt and started calling him Rosie. Only he and his troop knew that nickname until now, of course.

CHAPTER NINE

The timing of Mr. Heinz's arrival was perfect because we'd set a second meeting with the other parents for Sunday. I think they'd be surprised to see everything we discovered during the second trip to the cave. They probably wouldn't expect an art dealer and appraiser to be with us, either.

The gang and I got together Saturday afternoon for a meeting at Home Base. It was our first official meeting there. We made a list of questions we wanted to ask Mr. Heinz that evening. One question was related to Lava River Cave and the authorities. Would we tell them of our discovery and when? Another question was how would we find out who the rightful heir would be? That was the coolest part of this whole thing for the club. We would be a part of giving something to a family they never knew they had, sort of like an unexpected gift. Righteous!

We had a few legal questions and wanted everyone to know we were concerned for our safety. If others knew where the art was stored and who stole it, they would quickly try to come after us.

Well, maybe I watch too many old Bond flicks, but I found myself looking over my shoulder. *Honest.* Grandpa called it paranoia. I just called it having the creeps.

The meeting would take place at our house, so Grandpa secretly moved the painting from its hiding place at his ranch. Seeing the painting after only a few days still took my breath away. The gang and I stood in the den, staring at the Van Gogh with awe. If I could imagine what it might feel like to be in the presence of royalty, this might come close.

Meanwhile, Mom and Nana began cooking supper for the gang and family. As we headed out of the den, Delilah walked in. I tried to explain nicely that she shouldn't be near the expensive art. I reminded her that it didn't belong to us and that we were trying to find the family it did belong to. She listened and thought for a moment. She took my hand and whispered thoughtfully to me.

"Geez, Grandpa is right. You *are* paranoid. I only want to look at it, not play with it. Just because I'm six years old doesn't mean I don't know beauty when I see it, Chumlee."

You know, she was right. We stood together for about ten minutes. I watched her take in the painting the same way I had days before. Its beauty didn't know age. My little sister reminded me of something special that day. Beauty *truly is* in the eye of the beholder, no matter what age.

Mr. Heinz's plane landed earlier than expected that night. He and his assistant arrived shortly before supper and ate with us. He turned out to be friendlier and easier going than I imagined. I expected he would be stuffy and boring, but he was a real hoot! He and Grandpa told old war stories and kept it light, you know, no blood and gore. He told us about the day he first called Grandpa *Rosie.*

Mr. Heinz almost couldn't keep a straight face when he told us the whole company walked by Grandpa, one by one, saying, *GooD morning, Mr. President, Good morning, Mr. President.* Well, as expected, Grandpa laughed and was quick with his comeback! He nodded and reminded us that *Presidents don't do dishes.* Good rebound, Grand.

After supper, Dad, Grandpa, Mr. Heinz, and his assistant, Miss Walsh, retired to the study. Everything was displayed and laid out for the authentication process. Mr. Heinz also agreed to examine the tidbits of evidence, hoping he would give us his opinion. At the very least, he could tell us whether it seemed like the real deal.

Nana, Mom, and the gang played cards in the living room. Who were we kidding? We were ready to jump out of our skins; we were that anxious! Suddenly, the others walked down the hallway like a troop of soldiers. They looked serious and didn't say a word until Mr. Heinz pulled up a stool in front of us. He asked us to form a circle.

"I know how hard the wait must have been for you, and I completely understand, so I'll get right to it." I swallowed hard. "Miss Walsh has taken some samples to be processed back in Chicago. I don't expect receiving the results to take longer than a week. The tests will assist in further authentication." He scanned the room and smiled. "My assessment, in working toward total provenance, is that the painting is authentic." Our cheers erupted like our football team suddenly caught a Hail Mary pass! I quickly began asking questions.

"Oh, thank you, Mr. Heinz! I have a question: what is "provenance?" He smiled at me.

"Yes, it's pronounced *prah-ven-ance*. Provenance."

"Yes, provenance. Can you explain this to us?"

"Provenance" is a word that describes several different specific tools needed for full authentication. I've seen and studied Van Gogh's paintings long enough that his style, or aesthetic, is true. Miss Walsh took painting samples, which should help verify the date by materials used. One crucial part of provenance is documented ownership history." Mr. Heinz thought for a moment as a serious look appeared on his face. "This could be tricky, guys."

"Well ..." Tula hesitated. "What do you mean, tricky? How do we find out who it belonged to and where they live, or where their children live?"

"Good question, Tula. Thanks to Dean's father and Rosie, we've carefully examined the articles they brought back with them. They appear to have been dated sometime during World War II. Miss Walsh, who's fluent in several languages, is quite certain the scribble on the paper and brown bag are German."

"Okay," Spooky chimed in, "what does that have to do with Vincent Van Gogh?"

"Well, Spooky, it seems, by all accounts I'm aware of, 'The Painter on his Way to Work' was hanging in the Kaiser-Friedrich Museum in Germany when the United States bombed Germany during the Second World War." He paused for the bombshell. "This piece of art was documented to have been destroyed by fire in about 1945 during the airstrike, along with many more artifacts. This painting isn't supposed to exist any longer.

"Holy smokes!" It was only a matter of time before Jonas weighed in. "That, sir, is incredible. Neither the world nor the family heirs are aware it exists. Only those of us in this room?"

"Well, Jonas, in theory, but we must remember the painting was placed in the cave room by someone other than us. The questions we must address are: *who built the secret cave room? Who hid the painting there? who stole the painting?*" Jonas put his hand over his mouth. "Yes, the only explanation is that this painting was stolen. By whom, we don't know. If I want to complete provenance truly, we must find the answers to these questions or at least, eventually, put this into the hands of proper authorities."

"Which proper authorities, Mr. Heinz?" I asked.

"I'm not entirely sure right now. A lot depends on what we discover during our initial search through Bode-Museum historical documents. Years after the museum was restored, they renamed it after its original founder, Wilhelm von Bode. Anyway, one thing at a time. Let's process the other tests. In the meantime, I'll make a few general calls without spilling unnecessary beans. Are you kids in agreement? After all, this is *your* discovery." He smiled broadly. We all agreed, of course. "Let's all digest this tonight. I anticipate more questions tomorrow from the rest of your parents."

The gang and I met at Home Base to talk things through and try to make sense of all the new information. I was still stoked! My brain was working at a million miles per hour. New thoughts bounced around my head about bad people coming back to find the painting we took from Lava River Cave. It was exciting, but we also felt a little scared. The other club members and I have known each other for four years. We knew each other pretty well. We knew enough about each other to know we'd never back down from a challenge. Why would we start now?

Just as we were getting settled in the padded bench seats, we heard voices coming from the back of the house. I got up and walked out to the walkway to see who it was. I was shocked to see Miss Walsh and Ernie Heinz walking across the yard toward the tree house. Miss Walsh was carrying a plate of brownies, and Mr. Heinz was carrying ... wait for it ... a gallon of cold milk.

"Ahoy up there!" I heard Miss Walsh calling from the ground below. "How shall we approach?"

"Oh, hi, Miss Walsh!" I yelled down. "Just step onto the platform and, when you're ready, push the button. It'll glide you up to the balcony." I yelled back at the gang. "Hey guys, we've got freshly baked brownies and milk on the way!"

"Oh, dude, don't play with my emotion." Spooky was a brownie fiend, if there was such a thing. Geez, he actually started drooling. *Yuck.*

"Hello, kids. Thank you for granting us passage. We come bearing yummy gifts." We all cracked up laughing.

"Please come inside and join us. Grandpa would be pleased for you to see his handy work." After a few moments of exploring Grandpa's tree house, we sat down together. We expected they wouldn't be there only to deliver us brownies. Mr. Heinz broke the ice.

"You know, kids, there was something Miss Walsh and I wanted to discuss with you. Although it's a brief history lesson, it may somehow relate to our current situation with the Van Gogh. I think Miss Walsh can explain better."

"Thank you." She gazed out the window. She seemed to

be collecting her thoughts. "Have you ever heard the term or name *The Monuments Men*?" We all raised our hands as a yes. "And do you know who they were? Yes, Tula?"

"We all covered the basics in history class. We all remember a movie that came out a few years ago, but none of us saw it. We were a little younger."

"Alright then, I'll cover everything I know. Mr. Heinz, please feel free to interject." Again, she gathered her thoughts. She was well-spoken. Her words were easy to understand. "The Monuments Men were a group of men and women from thirteen nations. Most of them volunteered for service in the newly created group *Monuments, Fine Arts, and Archives,* or MFAA. Many were museum directors, curators, art historians, artists, architects, and educators. Are you with me so far?"

"Yes," Jonas whispered, "this is fascinating." Miss Walsh smiled at him.

"Together, they worked to protect monuments and other cultural treasures from the destruction of World War II. In the last year of the war, they tracked, located, and, in the years that followed, returned more than five million items stolen by Hitler and the Nazis." Spooky suddenly yelled in anger.

"Oh, those horrible creeps! How dare they steal things that were so special to those who owned them! Those creeps!"

"Yes, Bartholomew, I agree. These men and women not only had the vision to understand the greatest cultural and artistic achievements of civilization, but they joined the front lines to do something about it." Tula stood with her fist in the air.

"Yes! Fab!" Ernie and Miss Walsh giggled at her enthusiasm.

"We agree, Tula." Miss Walsh paused once again and

continued with a more serious look. She leaned forward and spoke softly to us. "Their job description was simple: to save as much of the culture of Europe as they could during combat." We all sat quietly for a few minutes. I said the only thing that made any sense to me.

"They were unselfish heroes. It was like their mission was personal to them. Miss Walsh, how many were a part of the Monuments Men?"

"I can't say for sure, Dean. My information says more than three hundred."

If you thought there were a lot of things floating around my head before this meeting, well, it was certainly jam-packed now—complete overload. We finished the brownies and milk after Miss Walsh and Mr. Heinz drove to their hotel rooms. We needed rest not just for our bodies but for our brains. There were so many possibilities swimming around in my noggin that I knew I had to try to put them out of my mind until morning.

This was more serious and much more complicated than we ever imagined. There remained a huge question mark over how this all ends.

CHAPTER TEN

When I woke up Sunday morning, I felt like I hadn't slept very well. I sat on the edge of the bed and dangled my legs for a while. It was raining outside.

I stared out my window at the rain for a long time and thought about the past week. This whole adventure still seemed like a dream. I actually tried pinching myself to see if it hurt or not. Nana Sarah once told me that if I pinched myself and didn't feel it, I must be dreaming. I felt it, and it hurt.

Don't get me wrong. I was thrilled to be a part of such an excellent adventure, and I was also jazzed about possibly finding an heir to accept the lost art. My problem was that I couldn't figure out how this all might happen. I knew, no doubt, that these were grown-up things. Sure, I knew the gang, and I would be front and center. I think I was waiting for Mr. Heinz's first move so I'd feel better about everything. That, and I was scared for our lives. I realized it on Sunday morning as I stared out my bedroom window at the rain.

I expected it would be an extremely busy day, so I forced myself out of bed and into the shower. Mom must have heard me because she had breakfast on the table when I got to the kitchen. She always seemed to do just the right thing at the right time. I guess it comes with growing up. I usually consider myself pretty spastic when it comes to stuff like that, but somehow, Mom and Dad always told me they were proud of me anyway. I looked over at her while she washed the dishes. She looked worried.

"Mom, the eggs rock! The French Toast is yummy, too. Thanks for the awesome breakfast." I tried to break the silence a bit.

She smiled back. "You're welcome, honey. I love the smell of the French Toast, you know, that cinnamon smell?"

"I'd like to know what the rest of the free world is eating for breakfast this morning because it ain't this!" We both busted out laughing.

"Good thing because I'm pretty sure I'd run short on eggs!" We both laughed again. She went back to her chores.

"Mom, is everything okay? You look a little, well, worried. I can see why you might be worried if it's about this whole stolen painting thing."

"I am, son, and I know you are, too. According to our discussions with Ernie Heinz, knowing how to proceed and what's right seems to be a fine line." She paused.

"You trust him, don't you, Mom? I mean, it's okay if you don't."

She smiled back at me.

"Actually, your father and I discussed the very topic of trust last night. We both trust Mr. Heinz and believe he has everyone's best interest at heart. We also know he would never do anything that would put us in danger, at least not intentionally." She wrapped her arms around me and gave me one of her award-winning hugs. "It's cool, son. We'll look back on this adventure one day and be glad we were part of it."

"I think you and Dad are right. It'll be an excellent adventure! Speaking of Dad, where is he? I thought I heard him leave in the middle of the night."

"Yes, he got called to pilot about three this morning. There's a bad burn on the south ridge of the plateau." No wonder she looked worried.

"Which ridge, Mom? There was a group of junior hikers and hike masters scaling that area this weekend. Does anyone know if they have returned yet?" I started to get worried, too.

"Is it one of your mentor groups, Dean?" She seemed more concerned than ever.

"I thought it was the Little Grey Knights, but I don't know f or sure. Spooky would know. He's the captain of that mentor group." I dialed Spooky and gave the phone to Mom.

"Hey, Mrs. Mandel. The Little Grey Knights were heading in the general direction of Sipapu, but not as far or high. So, it's on the side where the burn is. And, as far as I know, they haven't returned yet." My mom's eyes opened like saucers as she listened to Spook.

"Spooky, I know those hike masters, and I'm sure they're well equipped with talkies and supplies. I'll radio Dean's Dad and forward the information. Thank you!"

I heard her talking to Dad on the speaker phone, so I went over and joined her in the talk. So far, Dad verified that the kids and hike masters had been located in a cool zone between two burn sites. He mentioned that the distance was large enough for a safe rescue but that he could only spare a pilot and one rescue ranger.

"Deano, this is where you and Spooky come in. Because it's far enough away from smoke and fire danger, you two have been permitted to assist the ranger. You'll be helping to get the children line-attached to the ranger on the ground. I understand one of the two hike masters broke a leg." My adrenaline began pumping as I helped put the rescue plan in order.

Spooky's cell phone had been on speaker so he could hear the plan, too.

"Spooky, did you hear the whole telephone conversation? Do you understand the plan?" Spook was great at formulating plans carefully. One wouldn't think so by his aloof, hippy-like attitude. Somehow, it all worked. Without question, I'd put my life in Spooky's hands any time. I trusted him that much, even though he was a geek.

"Yeah, dude, I heard it all. My dad has been listening, too, because he always has to be prepared to give an official statement to the press. Being a senator has its weird stuff, right, dude?" He laughed using his best dorky nose snorting. "Now, let's get on with the plan. I'll be waiting outside for your car in, say, fifteen minutes?"

"That's a plan. Oh, and Spook, don't forget the heavy-duty boots. I don't expect heat, but there could be traveling soot. Got it?" I was in club leader mode now.

"Yes, oh exalted leader." I knew he was kidding, but just the same, I could do without his dramatics. I rolled my eyes, as usual.

The recent developments of the morning and the rescue

I was suddenly a part of put my head back where it belonged. Hiking, copters, Hotshot Crews, and the canyon life I was used to made me feel grounded for the first time in a week. From the moment we discovered the Van Gogh painting, that all went out the window. It felt like someone yanked the rug out from under me. At that moment, I didn't feel sure about anything. I *needed* this rescue. I *needed* to be a part of something I knew well. I felt like Dean again, and it felt good.

My mom and I picked up Spooky in front of his house. Senator Jordan was with him and spoke to Mom for a few minutes.

He smiled at us and said, "I'm proud of you kids. Now go get those junior hikers and bring them home!"

"Yes, sir!" we both chimed in together. I respected Spooky's dadas much as he did.

We drove for a while. I'm not sure how long, but it seemed like a long ride, especially when we were needed to help rescue stranded kids.

I spotted an opening in the field next to the Ranger's Station. The helicopter and rescue ranger stood waiting patiently for us.

Spooky looked over at me and outstretched his fist for a fist-bump.

"Let's do this, Deano!" He winked my way. I looked directly into his eyes.

"Let's go rescue some kids, brother." It was a fist-bump to end all fist-bumps.

We jumped out of Mom's car after her well wishes and hugs. We ran to the waiting copter.

The pilot addressed us by name as he read it from his

order sheet.

"Dean Mandel? Bartholomew Jordan?" We nodded and shook his hand. "Got your gear?"

"Yes, sir!" We both yelled over the loud, thumping noise of the helicopter blades.

"All right, buckle up, and let's go get those kids!" We pulled up seconds later. The ground got farther away pretty quickly. The pilot banked sharply right, and we were on our way to ground zero.

Meanwhile, Grandpa and Nana were at our house getting ready for the big meeting that afternoon. Mr. Heinz and Miss Walsh arrived early, too.

Mr. Heinz had been up much of the night talking to Germany. There was a nine-hour time difference, so he took advantage of it and called the Bode Museum. He was on the prowl for old records, particularly those that might have answers about the Van Gogh piece and its location during the World War II bombings.

It was fascinating, but so many years had passed. Who keeps this stuff? It seemed like a dead end to me. The paper trail probably ended when the painting was believed to be destroyed in a fire. To most people, the art would be gone, gone, gone.

Tula and Jonas were already at my house. They were my eyes and ears. Tula tried listening in on Grandpa and Mr. Heinz's conversations, but they quickly retired to the den, where the door stayed closed for a long time. Jonas figured if there were anything we needed to know, Mr. Heinz wouldn't hold back.

The meeting was pushed a bit later in the afternoon to give Spooky and me a chance to get home from the rescue.

Meanwhile, the conditions were a little worse at the rescue site than we imagined. Spook and I were asked to wear breathing masks as a precaution. The ranger was lowered down to ground zero first, where one of the hike masters was waiting. They talked briefly as they pointed to what looked like the direction of the kids and injured hike master.

The ranger looked up at the hovering copter and motioned to send us down. It was pretty scary because I'd never been lowered during an actual rescue. My past training came back to me quickly. Spooky was a real pro, and I let him take the lead because he was the captain of that mentor group. The kids all came running from behind their protective rocks, waving and calling Spooky's name. It was a nice sight to see.

"Captain Spooky, Captain Spooky! Yeah!" He just knelt and let the kids run into his arms.

"Hey, gang! Oh, so awesome to see you, dudes!" Spooky said, "I'm so proud of you boys! Are you all okay?"

Spook reassured the boys and talked with them away from the chopper. This made it easier for us to get the injured master onto the copter. He was in a lot of pain but somehow made it to his feet and used the ranger and me as his crutch. He was never so glad to see help arrive. The hike master looked at me and smiled before he was lifted to safety.

"Hey, Captain Spooky is the Senator's son, right?"

"Yes, he is, and I'm so proud of him and to be his friend." I was busting with pride.

"Yes, I can see why. He's going to make a great dad some-day." He patted my shoulder. I looked up and gave my thumbs up to retrieve the hike master. He was quickly whisked up to safety.

Without too much fanfare, the kids were quickly pulled up to safety. It was lucky for us that the wind had died down. Trying to move people on a copter cable in the high wind was scarier than heck!

Finally, Spooky, the ranger, and I were hoisted into the helicopter. Boy, was I glad that was over! We remained quiet while we listened to the completed rescue call to the Fire and Rescue Base.

"All survivors aboard and accounted for. One adult with a left leg injury. Making a drop at Flagstaff Medical Center via the front-side landing pad, then drop the remaining group off at the Ranger Station pad." A friendly response came back over the radio.

"Great job, and congratulations on a successful rescue to all. Well done!" We immediately broke out with cheering and clapping! We were happy the kids were safe.

We were so stoked and couldn't wait to tell everyone about our most excellent adventure. For the first time in a week, I felt ready and eager to confront the huge challenge waiting for me at home. I was ready to get this thing done *onward*, as Grandpa would say.

CHAPTER ELEVEN

All in all, we still managed to get back to my house before two o'clock. We were dirty, stinky, and hungry. Mom took care of the food. Spooky and I took care of the dirty, stale, smoky smell with long, hot showers. I was ready to face news from Mr. Heinz.

We only had an hour to catch up on the status of our delicate project. With the other parents arriving for a four o'clock meeting, there was lots to do. Mr. Heinz and Miss Walsh didn't waste a minute.

"Okay, no formalities. Let's get right down to business after we acknowledge Dean and Spooky for their willingness and courage in this morning's rescue mission. Congratulations on a great job!" Until that minute, I didn't realize how proud I was of the whole rescue crew and that Spooky and I were part of it.

"These are our mentor kids; we would do it again in a second." Spooky nodded in agreement. "Mr. Heinz, we can't wait to hear your news."

"After speaking to the curator of Bode Museum, he gave me a short list of World War II artifacts suspected to have either been stolen or hidden. It's possible some pieces were taken back by their owners somehow. Nevertheless, these suspicions are not based on pure truth. They're only possibilities. Having said that, the list of artists is awe-inspiring." I wondered how extensive the list could be.

"How many are on your shortlist, Mr. Heinz, and what does it mean?"

"There appear to be seven or eight. This painting is one from the list." We all gasped for a moment. "What it implies is that those works of art met the same demise that our newfound art had, which is that they were also stolen. The tricky part is: did the same party steal them and our Van Gogh? Perhaps. The curator further hinted that it may have been the work of a crime ring that posed as reputable parties. What that means is unclear. For now, we'll stick to this painting."

"What else, Mr. Heinz?" Tula inquired.

"Yes, what's next?" Jonas chimed in.

"The next question is how we go about finding a rightful heir. This is possible if we can access early records of the museum and, if not, the original Monuments Men records were kept in a diary documented by those who were privy to when the art might have been removed from Jewish homes. It could take some time, but there's no doubt we're closer than ever to provenance."

"Is there anyone else who may have information about possible heirs to the stolen art?" Nana Sarah spoke in a soft, emotional voice. The thought of placing the art with an heir choked her up a little. She didn't know it, but we were all choked up.

"There's one other group I got from the curator that I haven't checked on yet. I'll need Miss Walsh because of her fluency in many languages. The group claims to be able to assist in locating heirs to lost art. I don't know how reputable they are, and we'll check before we even contact them. The group's name is *New MFAA: Restoring Art to Heirs*. It might be a great source, and it may just be a dead end. So, let's get through today first." While we waited for the others to join us, we headed for the kitchen to eat snacks. Mr. Heinz grabbed me before I left the den.

"Dean, Miss Walsh, and I want to speak privately with the club after the big meeting. Is that okay?"

"Sure. What's up?" I was curious. He only said that it would be a surprise. I love surprises.

The meeting lasted almost two hours. Mr. Heinz and his assistant rehashed our earlier meeting and everything we'd discussed the day before. There were a lot of questions.

Mostly, everyone seemed surprised that Mr. Heinz had gotten to town so quickly. They seemed pleased that some authority overseas had at least been notified and put on notice. I don't think the museum was in a position to do anything but help us solve the puzzle.

Although Mr. Heinz hadn't covered it with us earlier, he mentioned contacting Coconino National Forest about the latest discovery at Lava River Cave would be a good time. My grandfather seemed confident that it could be handled quickly, and the focus was placed on jurisdiction from out of the country. The Bode Museum was in Germany, and Mr. Heinz acted as a go-between for the art. The authorities for Coconino would be busy taking pictures of the cave room and doing their own investigation. We would be out of it after we attended one last cave visit with them. It would be a blast!

Finally, at the end of the meeting, the gang stuck around in the den to see what Mr. Heinz and Miss Walsh had to say.

"Okay, kids, I'll turn this over right away to Miss Walsh. This plan is her brainstorm." She smiled and called us over to the overstuffed sofas on the other side of the den.

"When last we spoke of the Monuments Men, there was a lot of information to take in, wasn't there?"

"Yes, ma'am, you could say that." I smiled as I answered for the club. "We pretty much understood basics from school. The things you added were interesting, and we'd love to hear more!" The others agreed and chimed in, too.

"Well, that's good to hear. How about the story from beginning to end? We brought a copy of the film to watch. Talking about something is good; we can use our imaginations to fill in our visuals. Your understanding can sometimes be deeper when you see it in picture form. I think this will be well worth watching. What do you say?" We all chimed in together, a resounding. YES!

"Wonderful! Someone will come in shortly with supper. This way you can see this all the way through. When the film is over, we can discuss our situation and the possibility of what we face in reality. It'll make mountains more sense and may make you feel part of this."

The pizza arrived. The lights in the den were dimmed. The film began to play. I could speak for the gang when I say that our eyes never left the TV screen. We laughed when it was funny. We cried when it was not, especially Jonas. We sat quietly in the dark room together when the film was over, and the TV screen went black.

CHAPTER TWELVE

The last thing I remember thinking about Sunday night before I fell asleep was all that had happened in one short week. We still had another week of Spring Break. I couldn't imagine how we would possibly top last week. The sun wasn't up yet, but I heard birds chirping suddenly. *What the heck? It was my phone!* Okay, at 6:15, it better be good. The incoming ID said it was Tula.

"Hey what the heck are you doing up so early? Is everything okay?" I yawned loudly into the phone. Tula said I sounded like a wild coo-coo bird. Okay, whatever.

"Yeah, everything is okay, but I was thinking." She paused, and I grabbed my chance at a rebound.

"On purpose, or is it a freak of nature?" I laughed with my indoor laugh.

"Oh, you're a comedian, aren't you? Well, I thought if Mr. Heinz had told Lava River about the cave room, they would probably be interested in having us come out and show them the ropes, you know?"

"Mm, yeah. Go on."

"Well, now that we aren't sneaking around, I'd like to get pictures of the gang in the cave room. If we don't take the opportunity to do it now, we may not have another chance once they turn this over to bigger authorities. So, what do you think?" She sounded jazzed about her idea, and I was, too. It would be cool to have a picture like that hanging on my bedroom wall.

"Well, I'll call Grandpa to see if he knows when Mr. Heinz will be in his office. They went back to Chicago last night. Did you know?"

"Yeah, I figured they would. I can't wait to get the results of the samples they took from the Van Gogh. *Ah*, provenance." She drifted into Tula la-la land for a minute.

"Yeah, me too. Okay, I'll call you back a little later. Can you text Spook and Jonas to see if they'd be up for revisiting the scene of the crime?" We laughed. I guess we never considered our sneaky behavior as criminal, but the reality is that, technically, the Coconino National Forest Reps. *could* press charges if they wanted, but hey we're just a group of innocent kids, right? *Ahem.*

I learned later that morning that the proper authorities at Coconino National Forest had been notified. They'd already set up a meeting at Lava River Cave that morning for ten o'clock local time, and we, the gang, were, *how shall I say*, politely ordered to attend. Yep, gulp is right.

Grandpa and Dad were doing their best to be as agreeable as possible. One condition was that no press was allowed. They were not to be notified, and an informal hush-type agreement was in place. I wasn't even sure whether the gang could take photos. I would leave that up to Grandpa. All this new stuff was exciting and scary, too. Although we found a lost piece of art and history, we also knew we'd have to answer for our sneaking around.

Mr. Heinz and Miss Walsh were back in Chicago and received the test results from the painting. It was official that the Van Gogh painting was authentic! We were thrilled! Now we could move ahead with trying to locate a rightful heir. To do this, we would need to find out who the proper owners were at the time the painting was stolen from the museum. I was sure Miss Walsh was on that one like white on rice! *Wow,* I just sounded like Spooky. *Ugh.*

All the cell phones and our home phones were ringing off the hook. Some calls were from the gang's parents and others from Grandpa, Mr. Heinz, Lava River Cave officials, and I even think our lawyer called. All the parents agreed they would be present outside Lava River Cave with attorney representation. Mom told me it was to make sure the gang was protected. Nobody was expecting trouble, least of all me. Finally, Dad came into my room and told me it was time to go.

Jonas was texting me from his dad's car. *Hey, this is scary. I feel like I'm going to the principal's office.* I told him not to be scared. I looked at this day as a little historic because of what we'd learned about the Monuments Men and their crusade. Jonas wrote back. *I'm thinking about the MM film we watched last night. I feel honored, don't you?* I told him I did, too. Who knew a week ago that my club would be into this? Spooky texted me. *Dude, I'm freaking out, man! My Mom keeps saying, 'Bartholomew, do you understand what this all means?* I burst out laughing because his mom is such a sweet and supportive lady, and Spooky can be a real doofus! I just told him to chill out and be cool.

Finally, as I expected, Tula chimed in with a text. *Wow, Deano, is this all really happening? We're certainly getting a lot of attention by the looks of all those vehicles and flashing lights ahead.* I wrote her back. All I could think of to say was, *no kidding, 'Cuz.'*

Dad pulled up and stopped behind Jonas' car. The rest pulled up behind us in a row. Our family attorney rode with us in the car and spoke before we left. She encouraged us to relax and be as helpful and patient as possible. Let them ask the questions. Mom winked at me as we stepped out of the car. A gentleman wearing a big smile walked over and greeted us. By now, the gang and their parents stood in front of their cars, waiting to hear what he'd say.

"Good morning to all! Thank you for joining us. Let me start by saying that we're proud of the members of the Young Climbers Club for coming forward after what has likely been a *startling* week for you." We all laughed because the word startling seemed sort of appropriate. Other, more exciting words came to my mind as well. He continued. "The easiest way to proceed is for each club member and their parents to sign in at the small table. Afterward, we'll ask questions and brief you on how we'll proceed into the Lava River Cave. Any questions so far, folks? Okay, first up is Dean Mandel. Follow me, please."

For the first time, I felt like I was going to be interrogated. I wiped my sweaty palms off on my jeans. I hate sweaty palms. The woman seated at the table was older and quiet-spoken. She smiled, which made me feel more at ease.

"Hello, Dean. May I please have your signature on this

sheet? I'll answer any questions you have before joining your other club members at the table in front of the cave's entrance." My hand was shaking a little as I signed in. I couldn't think of any questions and was sure we would know pretty quickly how things would go down. "If you have no questions, you may say goodbye to your folks here and proceed to the gentlemen waiting at the table." I turned and looked at Mom and Dad. They smiled and nodded for me to follow the woman's instructions.

My legs felt like jelly. They didn't feel attached to my body. The table got closer with every step I took. The two men sitting behind it were *not* smiling. There were four chairs, I guessed, for each club member. Polite and brief greetings were exchanged between me and the official-looking dudes. I turned and saw Spooky heading our way, followed by Tula tightly holding Jonas' hand. It seemed mutual. I always felt Tula was protective of Jonas, like when he fainted in the cave room after seeing the Van Gogh for the first time.

"Good morning, kids. I'm Zach Duvall, and this is my deputy, Nate Brown. I'm an investigator sent by Coconino National Forest authorities to get your story as well as any facts you know now or before the discovery of the art." He looked up over the rim of his glasses. "Can any of you tell me whether you had any previous knowledge of this cave room or, more importantly, the art?" I think we all looked like deer staring into a blinding headlight. We couldn't speak. He smiled at us. "Okay, I got started on the wrong foot. You're *not* being accused of wrong-doing. You're among friends. We must know the facts and rely on you to inform us. This is exciting, but business first."

"I'm Dean Mandel, the club leader." I took a breath and continued. "It all started with Jonas here. He pointed out the dancing leaves. Then came the pink shoelaces, the tricky lever, and before we knew it we were standing in this room that opened up from, well, nowhere. Then we found the painting." He stopped me and smiled as he collected his thoughts.

"Let's start from the beginning. We need important points, like those you've made, without embellishment. Okay, please continue."

I continued, a little slower this time, to collect my thoughts. They were recording our meeting. Mr. Duvall invited me to make additions as often as I needed, even as we walked through the cave. We were told the recorder would run continuously, and the ten minutes it took to explain the important stuff seemed like two hours. Finally, Duvall asked if we could estimate the dimensions of the room. Spooky was a wiz at that sort of thing, so I volunteered his expertise.

"Oh, well, my best guess is that the room is about ten or twelve feet deep and about fifteen or so feet wide. We couldn't see anything until we got the gas lamp working." Duvall and Brown looked at each other and made some personal notes.

Minutes later, we were escorted to the cave entrance, followed by Duvall, Brown, Grandpa, Dad, and a camera operator from the investigator's team. I guess it was important to know the size of the room to see how many people would fit. Apparently, it was much bigger than they expected. Even then, there was a sense of disbelief coming from those who would follow us through the cave to the secret room.

As we'd done many times before, we had proper gear, lighting, gloves, and shoes. Everyone else seemed prepared except for the camera operator. Part way through the cave, he switched to his helmet cam so that he could free up both hands. Parts of the cave floor were known to be slippery and unsettled.

As we approached the end of the cave, I turned to everyone present and announced that we were arriving at the entrance to the secret room. Still, Duvall's reaction seemed calm, like he wasn't expecting much. He paused so that he could ask more questions.

"Now, Dean, what were you four looking for at this point? I mean, why were you really here? For all intents and purposes, this is a dead end." I sensed his interest peaked. This somehow tickled his curiosity.

"I mentioned earlier that Jonas and I had been at the top side of the cave, at its end, somewhere almost directly above where we are now. He saw a breach in the lava crust by way of the small crack where the air was rushing out. The air stream caught some leaves and threw them into the air. We were curious and thought that if we dropped something down that slim crack or hole, it would land here. It was basically a game, Mr. Duvall. A novelty." He looked curiously for a minute at the floor.

"Refresh my memory, Dean. What did you say you threw down the hole?"

"We borrowed a pair of shoelaces from Tula's backpack. Pink, to be exact." I threw Tula a quick wink. "Although I thought chances were slim, we hoped we might find them here, but we didn't."

"I see. How did you know no one would discover you and your science experiment?" He was clearly beginning to formulate the scene as it happened.

"Jonas had a walkie-talkie, and he watched the entrance

for the better part of an hour."

"All right then, Dean, let's continue. Please show us what you did next." I made an excellent suggestion at that point.

"Mr. Duvall, it would be a good idea if your camera operator took his place close to me and followed where I go and what I do if he expects to get the real good stuff." The camera operator didn't waste a moment and followed my lead.

"Oh? And what might that be?"

"I'm ready to open the door to the cave room if you're ready, that is." He looked startled for a moment and once again surveyed the tiny cave wall and floor. "Yes, by all means, then."

"Tula, could you please grab a glove from my pack? Thank you." I put the glove on snugly. "You see, Mr. Duvall, I was getting down onto the cave floor because I hoped the shoelaces would be somewhere on the ground in this area." I got down onto my belly as I had a few times before, feeling for the lever. "And there it is." I smiled and reached for the lever. Before I twisted it, I suggested they keep their eyes on the south wall. "Okay, everyone ready?" I heard Dad's voice in the back of the pack.

"Go ahead, son. Let it rip!" I reached in, twisted the lever, and with a rumbling shake, the door to the Lava River Cave secret room was opened! I sat up and looked at Duvall and Brown. Their mouths were open so wide I was sure they could've caught a few random flies in there. I giggled softly.

"Gosh, I love that part, don't you, gang?" They returned a collective, '*yeah!*'

From that moment, we all stood completely still. The only noise I heard was the random drop of water that dripped from the rock ceiling into a nearby puddle. Suddenly, the camera operator began snapping still photos. The clicking of the shutter release echoed down through the cave. It sounded eerie but cool. Without moving, my eyes darted to Tula, who shrugged. Next, I gazed at Spooky, who grinned his ever-*clever* Cheshire cat grin. He nodded my way and flicked his famous little Bic lighter.

"Is anyone in the mood for a little light?" Duvall spun around to see Spooky's Bic flickering against his flashy, plaid shirt. "I'll take that as a yes then. Jonas, can you assist, my friend?"

"With pleasure, oh lamp lighter." They chuckled softly.

Jonas helped to wet the wick with oil, and Spooky lit the lamp, which hadn't failed us yet! Oh, what a beautiful light it cast on the rock walls. It was golden and warm despite the damp, chilly air.

Without a pause, Tula and I joined the lamp lighters in the cave as though it was natural to us, as though we belonged. We did belong here. We turned slowly and faced the others. I spoke directly to the camera operator.

"Sir, would you please snap some photos of us? We very much want to remember this time and our discovery of the cave. These photos will be for our personal use only." Without hesitation, he snapped away. He walked slowly into the cave as he continued to snap the shutter.

I knew if I didn't ask for photos at that moment, Duvall and Brown might have objected.

Duvall moved cautiously into our cave room, trying to take as much as he could in. He was followed by Mr. Brown, who was scribbling notes. He turned and looked directly at me.

"This is remarkable. You *do* know that, don't you?" I

grinned and nodded. "The existence and building of the room is remarkable enough, but the historic notion, the implication, is enormous!" He paused and whispered, almost under his breath, *"Remarkable."* He looked around the room to get his bearings. "Where did you find the Van Gogh painting?" I walked over to the place near the oak barrel where the lamp sat.

"It was leaning against this wall. Oh, the pink shoelaces were found right where you're standing." Duvall looked down at his feet. "Dad? Could you and Grandpa please come here?" They came immediately and began explaining the items they found and removed. They knew much of the handwriting was in German and talked briefly about the notes on the brown bag. Miss Walsh translated the words, which talked roughly about a plan for storing art, but it was sketchy at best.

We spent almost two hours in the cave room while the investigating team took photos, measurements, samples, and anything else they could scrape up. We all needed fresh air, food, and a much-needed bathroom break! As we were leaving, Mr. Duvall put his hand on my shoulder and told me he was going to recommend this room be left open as part of the history of Lava River Cave. It would have to be resurveyed, photographed, and certified safe for visitors. The gang and I always felt safe there.

As we left the cave room, we intuitively knew it would be the last time as *our* cave room. I felt sad about that but was excited because I knew others would know our story and discovery. We understood that we needed to be available if any other questions should come up. As our research into finding a rightful heir would unfold, we were also expected to give the information to the authorities.

Exiting the cave, we saw our folks standing by, waiting patiently. There were lots of hugs going around. We were happy that part of our adventure was over. I was personally relieved. Being the club leader was tough because the discovery of our cave room depended on our secrecy. That didn't trump the cool factor, though.

We all piled into our cars and headed to Grandpa's, where Nana prepared a lunch feast. We relaxed and ate and talked about the next step in our journey. Grandpa and I stepped away and called Mr. Heinz. He was thrilled about the outcome and ready to begin our search for the painting's rightful owner. This would be the best part of our most excellent adventure.

CHAPTER THIRTEEN

The next couple of months flew by. It was just a blur to me. We were in the third week of May, and summer break from school was right around the corner. I spent most of my personal time doing extra practice and training with my climbing skills. Since I'd jumped to the thirteen/ fourteen competition age level, I knew I had to increase my stamina to meet the challenge. Back during spring break, I competed and placed very well. Unfortunately, it left me feeling exhausted. Thank goodness for me that Mom was a doctor. She helped me step up certain food groups to help my body grow strong.

The rest of the gang was doing pretty much the same thing, with the exception of two youth groups to mentor in junior hiking. My sister joined her first group the day after she turned seven. She was a real 'hoot!' Delilah could liven up even the most boring trail. The obvious, of course, was the long wait we'd had to hear any positive information about the Van Gogh's rightful owner.

Mr. Heinz and Miss Walsh spent the past couple of months following leads. Many of them seemed more like wild goose chases. The gang was losing hope for a successful end to this journey. It was Miss Walsh who usually picked us up and dusted us off. Her voice cheered us up instantly. She must have been a cheerleader during her childhood because she did a lot of cheering at her pep rallies! Miss Walsh was right when she told us that time would tell the truth about the painting.

Meanwhile, Grandpa started adding more benches in our new treehouse. He and a buddy from the Moose Lodge worked together some evenings when it was cooler. Hopefully, the new benches will be installed before the end of the week. Yes!

By Wednesday, I was stoked for the final bell to ring! I figured Grandpa would be done with the improvements in the tree house! I ran out to the curb and saw Dad parked and waiting for me. That meant that Mom was probably paged for an emergency or delivery.

"Hey, Dad, I didn't expect to see you. Do you know if Grandpa finished the tree house additions?" I saw this monster tree house go up from one pile of wood stacked near the tree's trunk a few weeks back. Now, the new benches? Yahoo!

"Yep, he sure did! He and a few buddies came this morning to drive in the final nails and wipe the last bit of stain off the wood. You're going to love his additions!" I clasped my hands tightly together and held them to my mouth to keep from shouting with excitement.

"I almost forgot, Deano. We have a couple of visitors in town." I was curious. Was it Uncle Danny and Aunt Deb? Aunt Sheila? "Mr. Heinz and Miss Walsh are back in town, and they have an update and some information for us."

"Do you know what this is all about, Dad?" I was surprised they appeared without any notice.

"Nope. Nada. I expect they hit on something positive and substantial, though. We've gone the last few months with dozens of dead ends and yards of red tape. Let's keep our fingers crossed."

"Does the gang know? Should they be there, too?" I was excited about possible news of our long-lost heir to the Van Gogh painting.

"Of course! Start texting, son! Tell them to be at our house about four o'clock."

Mrs. Falk, who was a schoolteacher, routinely picked Jonas up from school, but today, she also had Spooky and Tula in tow. It was a miracle none of us had practice events at any of our rock-climbing clubs that afternoon. We were all trying incredibly hard to be in shape for any upcoming competitions. As it turned out, everyone in the club was turning thirteen over the summer, so we would've had no excuses for not keeping up during an event.

As the others arrived, we did a lot of fist-bumping and high-fives. We were undoubtedly excited to hear some positive news from Mr. Heinz. The timing was good because we had all summer to work toward finding the legal heir to the lost Van Gogh if there indeed was one.

Our informal meeting began.

"It's good to see all of you. Miss Walsh and I have missed you."

Mr. Heinz stopped and shook his head in frustration. "Unfortunately, it's true that many of these past weeks were spent chasing wild geese. The good news is that now we know what direction *not* to go." He shuffled a few papers around and handed us photocopies of his new information.

"This is the only concrete information I have. I was sure I had checked this lead at the beginning of our search, but low and behold, this organization resurfaced out of nowhere. Moving forward, this group I mentioned in March is called the New MFAA, an acronym for Monuments, Fine Arts, and Archives, *Restoring Art to Heirs*. I've only had minimal contact with them, but it's positive."

"Mr. Heinz, how does their organization work? I mean, how can they find information when the Bode Museum that had all the original records couldn't?" I was curious.

"Good question, Dean. The Bode Museum admitted that all the records regarding ownership, even the existence of 'The Painter on His Way to Work,' were stolen when the art went missing. They then presumed that it likely met its demise in the fire. As a matter of fact, one positive and interesting factoid since March revealed that the museum admittedly discovered that the documents for the other several missing art pieces were gone as well."

A lot of oohs and aahs passed through the room and 'chatter' about Mr. Heinz's news. We were pretty sure we knew what this new information implied.

"Hey, Mr. Heinz, does this mean what we think it means? That all the paperwork was likely stolen, and all the art pieces were likely stolen as well?" Spooky was on to this quickly because he secretly suspected it was an art heist and crime ring from the beginning.

"Yes, Spooky. Although we can't confirm anything yet, it's entirely likely. I'm not sure this means anything to us.

We'd only have more information to give the New MFAA. In addition to this new tidbit, this organization probably has access to many more data-bases than the Bode Museum for its fact-finding work. For all we know, they use detectives to assist them." There wasn't much else to report. "So, any questions? If not, I'll get back to you in a couple of days, perhaps tomorrow, and let you know how we proceed on our search for our rightful heir. Agreed?"

"Yeah!" We were unanimous and happy because a fresh breath of life filled our hope and prospects for a happy ending.

We were all stoked and chatting up a storm about the new developments and were super excited to become part of this awesome, historic journey. Just as we were enjoying snacks and drinks in the living room, Spooky stopped in his tracks and slowly stood from the couch. His eyes never left the front window.

"Hey, Spook, what's up? What's got your attention? It's gotta be a chick!" Everyone burst out laughing, then I stood and saw the parade of black cars parked outside. "Holy crap!"

"Dude, it's a motorcade." He looked scared.

"Where did it come from? What do they want?" I was scared, too.

"Something's wrong. It's Secret Service." Just then, there was a loud knock on the front door. We heard the stern voice of a man announcing that he was Secret Service. Dad ran over and opened the door to them immediately. By then, we were all standing.

"Hello, Chief Warrant Officer Mandel. We're here to pick up Bartholomew."

"Is Bill, Senator Jordan, all right?" Dad was concerned

"We've received death threats for him and his family. Hopefully, we'll resolve this soon, but Bartholomew has to leave immediately for now." We all looked at Spooky as he went quickly with the Secret Service.

"I can't believe this is happening!" Tula was on the verge of crying. I put my arm around her shoulder.

"It'll be okay, Tula. This has happened before, and everything will be okay. It's usually a coocoo head looking to get attention." I knew better. This was a different world. With terrorism always a threat, I was *really* worried. Mom walked over with her cell phone.

"Lisa Jordan just texted me." She read Mrs. Jordan's note.

"Everyone is okay, and we will be going to an undisclosed location until it's safe. There are already leads on the threat makers, so, fingers crossed, we should be home by tomorrow. Spooky is a bit shaken up, but his father is good at calming him down, usually with a challenge of checkers or chess! Gonna be a long day. Love to all."

We were a little relieved after Spooky's mom texted us. Everything would be okay. The Secret Service knew how to do their job right. Spooky will be relieved when Senator Jordan's term is over.

We spent the rest of the evening talking about terrorism, hate groups, and what they do. After Dad's special operation regarding Bin Laden and Dad's rank increased from Chief Warrant Officer 3 to CW5; I was frankly surprised he hadn't gotten called back, what with terrorism and all.

Hopefully, I was wrong about that. Hopefully, my father would never face that, for all our sakes.

CHAPTER FOURTEEN

I imagined all the benches and storage cabinets in the tree house would have the beautiful look of a hand-finished boat. I trusted Grandpa to take all the time he wanted. I couldn't wait for Spooky to see it. What an awesome gift!

The next morning, I received a text from Tula reminding me that her grandmother was arriving from Finland at the end of the week. I'd never met her 'Mummo' before. I guess that means Grandma. A few summers ago, Tula's whole family went back to Finland to visit her. The pictures she took were gorgeous, and I couldn't wait one day to visit Europe myself.

The gang was excited to meet her. In the meantime, knowing the Jordans couldn't contact anyone, we waited impatiently for any word from Spooky. We still had two more days of school before the weekend. I had a feeling it was going to be a long two days.

Focusing on schoolwork that Thursday was nearly impossible. The last thing I needed to do was fail a quiz or a test. My grades would go south from there. It turns out I aced the quiz, but I knew I had to be careful till the end of school. My grades were important to me. During lunch, I went to my locker to grab my cell phone. When the screen lit up, I noticed a text from Mom. She was happy to confirm that Senator Jordan and his family were released from protective custody and had been cleared to go home! Outstanding! No doubt Spooky's first stop after returning home would be our house to be with the gang. I was sure he'd offer all the dirt he could muster.

Mom had snacks ready for us when we got home and made some cupcakes, especially for Spooky when he arrived. How did a doctor have time to make cupcakes? Mom always told me there was nothing to it. I knew better. The gang and I quickly finished our homework, not only to spend a little time with Spook, but Miss Walsh was stopping by with a brief update. Today was a good day.

We all paced back and forth across the living room impatiently, waiting for Spooky to arrive.

Suddenly, screaming like a girl, Jonas ran to the front door.

"Spooky is here! Spooky is here!" Jones gave him an expert bear hug as soon as he crossed the door frame. "We're glad you're okay, Spooky!" Tears dripped down his cheeks. I rolled my eyes.

"Wow, dude, easy does it! You'll crack a rib! I was only gone one day." He stopped in his tracks and gently sniffed the air. "Is that chocolate I smell? Mrs. M., surely you didn't have time to make me your famous chocolate cupcakes, did you?" She smiled at him. "I mean, surely, *somewhere* out there, some lady must be in labor. How do you do it, Mrs. M.?" He giggled as he strutted toward the cupcakes with his best Spooky swagger. "Oh my, and there they are. Come to Papa."

We laughed our butts off! It was good to have "the Spook" back. Suddenly, we heard a woman's voice. Miss Walsh peeked her head in from the front door.

"Bartholomew, you wouldn't begrudge an old British lady just one of your scrumptious cupcakes, would you?" She startled him as he spun around quickly.

"Anything for you, Miss Walsh. I'll share my cupcakes if perhaps you share some good news with us?" What a ladykiller. What a brilliant mind. What a doofus.

"Hi, Miss Walsh!" Everyone greeted her in unison. We were, after all, a club.

"I have some new information for you, but I was worried about Spooky and his family. What happened, Spooky? Are you all okay?" Miss Walsh sat close to him on the sofa while they shared cupcakes.

"All I can tell is that I'm glad it's over. Officials told us that this crazy dude had an impressive arsenal in his slummy apartment. He was crazy, man. He wasn't a terrorist or related to Radical Islam in any way. He was your garden variety nut case.

The weird thing is that he wanted my father to hire him privately to spy for him, to help him get foreign secrets. Why he thought my father would *ever* dream of such a ridiculous thing is insane! He was obviously going to use my father for wicked deeds, no doubt."

"It sounds like Homeland Security and the FBI did their jobs well and quickly." Miss Walsh patted Spooky's arm. I saw something I hadn't seen Spooky do in a long time. He cried, and then he hugged Miss Walsh. The gang and I huddled around for a group hug, ending in big smiles. What a day.

Spooky climbed onto the floor with us, and we sat around in a tight circle in front of Miss Walsh sitting on the couch. It was like another scene from the Sound of Music!

"Well, gang, let me begin by telling you that the information is slow to come, and there isn't much, but it is a bit raw and powerful. Hold on to yourselves." We all gasped lightly and leaned in closer. We couldn't take our eyes off Miss Walsh.

'The Painter on His Way to Work' belonged to a couple named Albert and Olga Rosen. They were a Jewish couple who, supposedly, donated their Van Gogh to the then Kaiser-Friedrich Museum sometime in the early 1940s." She paused briefly. "According to the New MFAA organization, they died during World War II." She paused again, "There were no children." Jonas gasped the loudest.

"Oh no, Miss Walsh! How did they die?" Jonas pressed his finger to his lip to keep from crying.

"Adolph Hitler had them executed." She leaned back against the couch cushions and took a deep breath. It was all so sad and disappointing. We sat silent for a few minutes, trying to digest this shocking information. Jonas broke our silence.

"Miss Walsh, how does this organization know Hitler murdered the Rosen's? How do they know the Rosen's didn't have any children?" Jonas was an emotional young man, but he was possibly the smartest of us in the club, with Tula a close second. Heck, none of us were schlubs.

"Well, I can tell you they claim to have gotten the information from the Bode Museum records. They claim the records listed no children as heirs by the Rosen's. I'm not sure about the Rosen's demise, but the organization claims they have diaries left by those close to Hitler, confidants, as it were, copies of those the Monuments Men may have used to find stolen art."

We let our minds go back to the movie we'd seen a short time back about the Monuments Men. The mention of a diary that listed much of the stolen art sounded familiar. Jonas continued as we watched with bated breath.

"Mr. Heinz told us about the records for this Van Gogh painting disappeared, the museum believes, at the same time the art disappeared."

Miss Walsh nodded, affirming that fact. "So, right now, we can't know for sure about the alleged listing of no children, but let's assume it's true. What would be the next step? Where would the Van Gogh painting hang?" Miss Walsh thought carefully for a moment.

"Well, I have to think about that, but it may be fair to say that your club may be able to make that recommendation, provided the donation is not to any private party but rather somewhere it may be enjoyed by the masses." She thought for a moment, and a look of brilliance crossed her face. "A place like the Holocaust Memorial Museum in Washington, D.C."

"That would be fair, I guess." Jonas looked as disappointed as we all felt. "And what about the claim of having been murdered by Hitler? What do you think, Miss Walsh?" We continued to listen intently to Miss Walsh and Jonas.

"Well, Jonas, I'll tell you it was entirely possible. I might even go so far as to say that *perhaps* the painting wasn't donated to the now Bode Museum by the Rosen's. *Perhaps* it was stolen from them like so many other Jewish families. Hitler's regime may have hung the Rosen painting in the Museum to conceal the fact that it was stolen. It's very sad indeed."

I finally chimed in. "What do we do now, Miss Walsh?"

It didn't sound to me as though this information was totally reliable.

"It's worth doing some digging, especially back at the Bode Museum, to see if they can possibly confirm or deny any of this information. I'm not hopeful. One thing is certain: the folks at the Bode Museum are on our side. They're in awe of your club and how you've handled this whole adventure. Mr. Heinz and I are proud to be acquainted with you. You're fine and valued people." Yup, another fist bump fest, this time with Miss Walsh.

CHAPTER FIFTEEN

Friday couldn't come soon enough. I could speak for the gang when I say we were on pins and needles waiting for updates from Miss Walsh. Realizing only one day had passed, I tried to put it out of my mind. Instead, I busied my mind with the excitement that Tula's grandmother had flown from Finland that afternoon. I looked forward to finally meeting her!

As I headed for my locker after the final bell rang, I received a text from Tula telling me her Mummo had arrived safely. Tula said she was all smiles but noticed she'd lost a little weight. She tried not to make any big deal about that. Neither did I. I was sure those two had a lot to catch up on. Tula told me all about the delicious, slapped ears she made for her 'Mummo.' Oh, slapped ears translates to cinnamon buns. Slapped ears are easier to remember.

"*Olen kaivannut sinua Mummo!*" (I've missed you, Grandma!) Tula exclaimed.

"And I've missed you as well, Tula." Her Mummo was

enjoying Tula's wonderful, slapped ears. She continued. "Tula, I am sick. I have cancer." Tula stopped chewing her food and stared blankly at Mummo.

"Oh, Grandmother!" Tula couldn't believe what she'd just heard. Did her mother know this?

"I have had a lot of treatment." She didn't look up from her slapped ear. Tula took a moment to absorb this shocking news.

"Are you in pain, Mummo?" She looked up and smiled at her granddaughter.

"No. Now I am here to heal." Tula sighed in relief as she smiled back at her Mummo.

"*Mita voin tehda?* What can I do? I will do *anything*!" Tula exclaimed eagerly.

"I need your love to help me heal, Tula." They smiled, and both hugged each other very tightly.

"So, do I have a deal?" Tula clapped her hands and giggled.

"*Kylla!* Yes! Yes! It's a deal." They giggled while they licked their sticky fingers.

Later that evening, I rode my bike to Van Hanen's house to meet Mummo. The house had a festive mood to it. It was filled with the beautiful smells of Finnish food and the sounds of laughter. What a lovely lady. I understood why Tula was so close to her. Her grandmother had the kind of spirit that drew a person in without understanding how or why.

Afterward, Tula walked me outside and shared the news her grandmother had given her earlier. At first, she didn't say or do much, but then she cried. She cried for a long time, and I held her for as long as she needed. My friend. My sister. I cried with her.

Later, I rode my bike slowly home.

CHAPTER SIXTEEN

Early Saturday morning, after a restless night's sleep, I called Grandpa. I thought of nothing, but the information Miss Walsh gave us a few days earlier. The thing that bothered me most was deciding whether to release the Van Gogh painting to the organization we knew as Restoring Art to Heirs. So far, they hadn't asked for the painting, but I knew it was a real possibility.

Part of me wanted to release it because I didn't feel worthy enough to have such control over a great historic piece of art like this. On the other hand, I didn't know enough about these people to trust them. Our club discovered this lost art, and I knew we all felt protective over it and its well-being. From what we learned so far, this poor piece of art has seen the likes of horror, despair, and thievery. This painting deserved the protection we promised when we found it. Our club's oath stated, "We are bound by our good words and committed to truth."

After breakfast, Grandpa picked me up with Delilah in tow and headed to his ranch. I asked if he would unlock his vault so I could sit with the Van Gogh art for a while. He knew what was going on and never asked for an explanation of my request—tough decisions called for time and careful consideration. So far, in my short life, big decisions have also called for logic from the brain and intuition from the gut.

I continued to study the art carefully as though I was memorizing each brush stroke. Every so often, I recalled snapshots of memories from our discovery at Lava River Cave. The impact of this whole adventure continued to grow. It was crystal clear how important it was to see this through to the end. As far as I was concerned, the club acted as stewards to the art, and I wasn't prepared to release it to anyone except its rightful heir or our permanent choice of display.

I said a quick prayer, and before I left the room, I turned one last time and spoke under my breath, hoping Vincent Van Gogh might hear me. I said, *You know, Mr. Van Gogh, this has been a real trip! And the honor has been all ours. I wish you could speak to us. We're lost and don't feel much hope. I believe in God, you know, and also in a little bit of cosmic fate. If you could send a message, that would be great!* I stopped because I knew how ridiculous that sounded, and I said as much out loud, *"Oh, this is so stupid!"* Suddenly, I heard Delilah's voice behind me.

"No, it's not, Dean. Your request isn't stupid at all." Delilah had walked in and heard my plea to Vincent Van Gogh. Awkward! She stood next to me and took my hand. She admired the painting and smiled. "You asked for a sign or an answer. Now it's out into the universe. You have to be patient and pay attention."

"Delilah, how in the world did you become such a clever and wise little girl? You're absolutely right."

"Grandma calls me an old soul. I think it means I'm wise for my age. Am I Dean?" She looked up at me with her pools of green eyes.

"Well, I can't explain it. It's almost like you've been here before. Or like you see the world through more experienced and accepting eyes." I tried to explain the best I could.

"Oh," was all she said. "So, the answer could come at any time. Pay attention, bro."

"To what?" I answered. I didn't do well with the cosmic world.

"Everything. Anything. And trust your gut. That's what Grandpa always says." She grinned at her clever observation.

"Um-hm. Yes, he does." She turned and left the vault room. She was right. This wasn't stupid. I left a parting shot. *Vincent, your beautiful art is safe with us. We promise.* Jonas shared more Van Gogh quotes he liked. I could only recall one. I turned one last time to speak to Vincent. *My friend Jonas is a great admirer of your work and your life. I'm his humble student. He shared one of your quotes that I like. 'I dream of painting, and then I paint my dreams.'* I stood still for a moment, then said goodbye.

As Delilah and I sat catching up with Grandpa and Nana Sarah, a SKYPE call came in on their laptop. It was Mr. Heinz. Wow, this was perfect timing! I hoped he had some additional information regarding the painting.

"Hello, Rosie! How is everyone doing? Let's see, who's there with you? Ah, Dean and Delilah. What a treat. Oh, hello, Sarah. You're looking well."

"And you also look well, but more than that, you look happy. Cheshir- grin happy. What's up?" Nana knew Mr. Heinz pretty well.

"Ha, yes. I have some news, and it's big. I communicated with my contacts at the New MFAA organization, and they tell me they've found a living heir to your Van Gogh painting! I know our original Intel was that the Rosen's had listed <u>no children</u> on their museum documents, but that may have been incorrect for several reasons." He tried treading carefully because he still lacked verification.

"Oh, *holy cannoli*, Mr. Heinz! If it's true, it would be the beginning of the end of this adventure. What's your opinion, Mr. Heinz? Any thoughts you can share?" I was hoping he might offer a glimmer of possibility or hope.

"Dean, I have to remain neutral and keep my thoughts and feelings to myself until you've viewed the interview. I taped it on SKYPE and am in the process of sending it your way. I want you to view this through completely unbiased eyes." I understood. It made sense.

"I just heard the incoming file 'ding' on Grandpa's laptop. Will you be available if Grandpa and I call you back after we look at your interview with the supposed heir?" I was eager.

"Of course, but before you watch it, I'll give you a little set up on who he claims to be. He claims to be Leonard Rosen, grandson of Albert and Olga Rosen from Germany. That's all I need to tell you. The rest will be on the tape. The good thing is that the interviewee speaks reasonably good English, so you shouldn't have any problems understanding him. The initial interview is about ten minutes long. If you've no questions, enjoy and speak with you soon."

Grandpa set up four chairs around the kitchen table with the laptop screen in the middle. Delilah was excited to witness the interview, too. Nana preset the volume and pressed the play button.

Suddenly, a gentleman who looked about fifty or so sat in the chair across from the camera. I could hear a lady's voice in the background. Although we didn't see her during the video, she sounded like she was giving him instructions. The woman's name was Hilda Wilhelm, granddaughter of Hans Wilhelm. Hans was one of Hitler's confidants back in the day. Ugh, that thought creeped me out. She represented MFAA.

The interview began with Mr. Rosen sharing a photograph of his late grandparents, Albert and Olga Rosen. The photo appeared to be old in black and white. It was yellowed around the edges. So far, it looked authentic.

"Hello. My name is Leonard Rosen. I am the grandson of Albert and Olga Rosen. This picture shows them sitting in their kitchen back in Germany." The interview was taking place at the New MFAA office in Brussels, Belgium. He continued. "They died during the war at the hands of Adolph Hitler. I don't know why they hung the Van Gogh painting at the Kaiser Friedrich Museum and stated they had no children. They had one son, my father Albert, Jr. Then, my father had one son, which is me. I have no brothers and sisters."

The interview continued with only a few random questions, and then it was over. The grandson appeared uncomfortable. I was unimpressed. Grandpa looked at me, and I looked at him. It was a stare-down for a minute, and then I broke the silence.

"So, what do you think, Grandpa?"

He grinned broadly. "Beauty before age." I loved his wry

sense of humor. I gathered my thoughts and glanced at a few notes I made.

"I don't buy it. Something wasn't gelling. It annoyed me that the Hilda Wilhelm lady didn't sit in a chair nearby and ask him the questions. I don't know. She seemed intentionally hidden from the camera." Grandpa nodded. "Now, it could be me, but the guy, what's his name? Leonard Rosen? He never looked emotional at all. Not when he talked about the grandparents and not when he talked about how they died. I'm not kin to any of this, and even I tear up at the thought of how the Rosen's died. Is there a copy of the still photo of the Rosen's we can have?"

"Well, Dean, I'm with you. I don't buy it either. Rosen seemed strangely uncomfortable. Not because he was overcome by emotion but because he seemed almost uncomfortable making his statements. I also agree with what you said about how unemotional he seemed about the whole thing. I would have cried if I found out my grandparents left me a Vincent Van Gogh painting!"

"I'm with you, too, Dean." Delilah chimed in. I had to ask her, just so she would feel included, what her thoughts were. "Well, I'd like to see the photo up close, too. Know why?" We all shook our heads. "Well, it's like this. I looked at the picture of the 'Rosen's.' At first, I thought there was a fingerprint on the lower part of his left eyeglass. No, wait, if I see it on the left, it's his right, right?"

We smiled and nodded. "Well, it looks more like a light-reflecting, but not any light. It glows in a funny way that I've seen before. Promise you won't laugh at me?" We all promised, crossed our hearts, and put a stick in our eyes. "It looked just like the light from a cell phone. Hey, I'm only seven, but I'm pretty sure there was no such thing as a cell phone."

Grandpa texted Mr. Heinz immediately, and he sent the still photo that was used in the video interview. We all took turns staring at the photo. Delilah showed us where she questioned the reflection, and, low and behold, we saw it. It was a white-blue hue that only came about during the recent technology age. The dadgum photo was *a fake*! So, it seemed, was Leonard Rosen.

It's likely that whoever posed as the Rosen's in this photo stupidly left their cell phone on the table just outside the camera frame. It was a good thing we questioned the whole thing because Mr. Heinz told us they wanted to take possession of the painting!

No, sir, we didn't buy it at all.

It turns out that Mr. Heinz was in total agreement with our suspicions and findings. He told Delilah he owed her the biggest banana split she could handle! For a seven-year-old girl, old soul or not, she could eat her weight in food! I hoped he would bring his checkbook to pay for it.

Mr. Heinz and Miss Walsh had a plan that they recommended we follow. We were eager to hear the plan and trusted his direction and experience. The SKYPE tone came in again. Miss Walsh was still in Arizona, so she used her checkbook to pay for it.

Mr. Heinz and Miss Walsh joined us at the table.

"Okay, folks. This apparent charade of theirs comes with some serious implications. For now, I recommend that we not 'let on' to Hilda Wilhelm and her brother Artie that we suspect they're fakes.

We stand the chance of losing them. Why would this matter? If we expect them to be the possible rotten apples or part of the art heist and crime ring, we need to go along to see what Intel we can get. First, I need a current photo of Hans Wilhelm's two grandchildren. They're proving the apple doesn't fall too far from that rotten tree!"

"Mr. Heinz, I know I probably watch too many spy movies, but don't you think it's possible that the man who posed as Leonard Rosen is actually Artie Wilhelm?" I hated to think the worst of people, but we had no other choice. "Also, don't you think it's possible that Leonard Rosen doesn't exist? That there is no grandson?" I felt like a clever super sleuth.

"Yes, to both, Dean. We can confirm the first suspicion easily as soon as we find a photograph of Hilda and Artie. Sadly, there may not be any grandson, real or fake."

I felt sad about that.

"Then we're right back where we started, without an heir. What information do you hope to get from the Wilhelms if they aren't good to us, Mr. Heinz?"

"Well, if they turn out to be fakes and they also turn out to have other motives, for instance, attempting to acquire the Van Gogh painting, then we can tie them to the possible crime ring that has nefariously been passed down from Hitler's regime and Hitler's confidant, Hans Wilhelm himself. In short, it might answer questions to the other half dozen pieces of art that went missing."

I turned and whispered to Grandpa. "What does nefariously mean?" He grinned and whispered back.

"Nefarious means evil, criminal, malicious, wicked." Oh my, that was a bad list. I dug the word, though. I decided it might become one of my new favorite words. Nefarious. Grandpa spoke up with a clever idea.

"Ernie, might I suggest some glances at the European newspaper archives for any photos of Hilda and Artie? In particular, the Belgian newspapers. Maybe they were featured when they announced the new organization. It's worth a shot." Mr. Heinz agreed.

The rest of the day was a real downer. The thought that Leonard Rosen might be a totally made-up person, right down to the name, was a bummer. I hoped there was a real Leonard Rosen out there, but I didn't expect anything good to come of this *nefarious* effort. I loved that word.

The upside to all of this, as Mr. Heinz mentioned, was that they were communicating with us. The more we pretended to trust them, the more comfortable they would become. A scary thought regularly crossed my mind: what if these people turned out to be as evil as their grandfather, Hans, legendary confidant to Hitler? That thought scared me half to death.

CHAPTER SEVENTEEN

Finally, we were into the last week of our school year! What a year it had been. The gang and I were jazzed about middle school. Although we hung out a lot with seventh and eighth graders at competitions, it'll be a nice change to be away from first and second graders—no offense toward my little sister, Delilah. Just like every school year so far, the last week crept by as though time was ticking backward.

I usually went to my locker a few times a day to check messages on my cell phone. It never interested me in having it permanently glued to my body. Next to all the exciting things I do in my life, my cell phone was pretty far down the list.

Unexpectedly, I had a text with an attachment. The text was from Grandpa, and it read: *Look what we found! A great photograph of Hilda and Artie Wilhelm taken only six months ago. Doesn't Artie look just like Leonard?*

I stared at the newspaper photo for a long time. I decided I would grab my sandwich and then head to the library. I wanted to see if I could rustle up any information on Hans Wilhelm. I needed to know how his two grandchildren were raised to become such horrible, greedy monsters.

Later that afternoon, I shared the newspaper photo with the gang and got immediate responses from everyone at the same time.

It was unanimous that they were deemed 'those nefarious scoundrels'! I did love that word. We decided to meet quickly at Jonas' house, which was central for all of us. I told them what I had found out at the library. It gave us an idea of how ugly the lives were of those inside Hitler's regime.

Hans Wilhelm was close to Hitler during his rise to power, especially during his fall of leadership. Hans was personally responsible for talking Hitler out of committing suicide.

The end result, of course, wasn't what Wilhelm had planned on. Many believed he was ready to steer Hitler toward another immense takeover. Thank heavens that never came to pass. As a personal note about Hitler, I found he learned to play piano as a teenager but was never professionally trained and accomplished.

Too bad the beauty of music didn't triumph over the historic mass murderer he chose to become.

Finally, the last bell of the school year rang on our final half-day. I received my report card, all A's, of course. We raced to my house because Mom had planned a gathering of our club and parents, complete with yummy food! Mr. Heinz and Miss Walsh had returned from Chicago with a new update. Grandpa was the only one who knew what it was all about.

After bragging about our report cards and grabbing our snacks, we headed back to the den for our meeting. I was surprised to see the Van Gogh painting on an easel, covered by a velvet drape. I was getting worried. Finally, Mr. Heinz began the meeting.

"Well, everyone, this has been an interesting several days since discovering that the Wilhelm grandchildren were fakes and potential thieves. More important, they've begun to trust us. I told them how impressed we were with how quickly they interviewed Leonard Rosen, or who we first believed to be Rosen. I also promised that we would be willing to ship the Van Gogh to them if they provided us with more information regarding their association. Our request, in particular, was for the names of the previous heirs to whom their lost art was placed, especially important being the name of the artwork. I want to see if it matches our list of stolen pieces from the museum."

I interrupted Mr. Heinz to object to sending our painting. "But, Mr. Heinz, why would we let go of the Van Gogh? We know we'll never see it again. I imagine we would never get the information you requested from them either." I was sure my face looked as pale as it felt. Mr. Heinz smiled at me.

"Dean, I understand your reluctance to follow through, but my plan is much more devious than that, right, Rosie?" We all laughed because we knew Mr. Heinz well, and when Grandpa had his hand in it, we knew we could trust it. "You see, I spent some time staging some shots of the real painting as it was being loaded into the packing crate, which is fake. Rosie and I had to mockup the shipping paperwork to produce it for them. The actual painting hasn't been loaded yet." He walked over to the covered painting on the easel and prepared to reveal it. "This is what they'll get when they finally receive the crate."

He winked and dramatically removed the cover, revealing a painting of Bozo the Clown! You'd never heard such laughter. The loudest, of course, was Spooky and his father, the senator, both hearty laughers.

"Mr. Heinz, where did you ever get that painting of Bozo?" Tula squealed between her belly laughs.

"Finding a print wasn't too hard. It was textured a bit and then fit into a fake copy of the frame on the Van Gogh. This is the final product. I know it won't be ex-rayed because of the sensitive nature of this historic painting." We all burst into laughter again. It seemed cleverer and sneakier than I *thought* Mr. Heinz could ever be. Somehow, I knew my grandfather had his hand in this as well.

"This will buy us time. If we can disprove their new information about a recent heir and the location of lost art, we'll be able to associate them with a crime ring. Even though the paintings were stolen decades ago, their existence is absolute, even though they haven't been recovered yet. They believe they're so close to getting this Van Gogh that they can almost. taste it."

"How long will it take for Bozo to arrive in Belgium, Mr. Heinz?" Tula wanted to know how long we had to stall the crooks.

"It gets packed tomorrow and will take one week. They expect it to be shipped, and we must provide them with the proof tomorrow. This will buy us a week to, hopefully, trap them."

This nefarious plan was beginning to 'get good.' I love a little tomfoolery.

CHAPTER EIGHTEEN

Living near the Grand Canyon and in the Coconino National Forest created rough living conditions. At certain times of the year, our area is prone to wildfires, some of them pretty nasty. The season could last up to six months. The best way to prevent small burns from exploding into full-blown, widespread forest fires was to have Hotshot Crews and Smokejumpers from the Fire & Aviation Management nearby.

I mentioned earlier that grandpa and Nana converted their barn into seasonal housing for these hard-working crews. Most Hotshot Crews consisted of twenty members. They were often called Type 1 Crews, but they were more than that since they exceeded the experience, training, and physical fitness required for a Type 1 Crew.

They're sent anywhere in the U.S. to fight wildfires. Tools of their trade included chain saws fuses, which were better known as cone-shaped pulleys, pumps, and engines, and understand and practice safe helicopter operations. The

Hotshot Program participated in physical fitness and conditioning programs, passing all necessary tests. Grandpa told me a typical fitness test required the person to perform a three-mile hike with a forty-five-pound pack in forty-five minutes. Yikes! The Young Climbers Club was in great physical fitness for our age, but the demands of these fire crews made us look unworthy.

The crews began arriving at Grandpa's compound before the end of May. Many crews would stay six weeks or so and rotate throughout the season. There were enough beds and shower facilities to house two twenty-person crews at a time. In addition, there were two long tables and a full kitchen for preparing meals, complete with two large refrigerators for a constant supply of cold drinks. Now I understood what kept Nana Sara and Grandpa so young! God bless them for their good work and service. They didn't think that way. They just enjoyed the heck out of the season.

For the third year in a row, my club went to Grandpa's ranch to help in any way we could as the crew got settled. Each bed was freshly made and came with two towels, washcloths, and a personal bar of soap. These folks may bunk together, but having to share toiletries was not cool. To top this off, Nana always had the fridges loaded with fresh sandwiches, salads, and fruit. Her food never went unappreciated.

CHAPTER NINETEEN

There was no doubt that Mr. Heinz was right to cooperate with the scoundrels because it bought us time, and they gave us more information than they realized. The time clock started, and we wasted no time. Miss Walsh gave each of us a checklist of things to eliminate as possible sources of answers or, sadly, dead ends. The time difference between Belgium and So, school was out, and the fire season was officially underway.

Mr. Heinz and Grandpa succeeded in getting the Bozo painting shipped to Belgium. As they drove away, bound for the shipping company, the gang and I waved goodbye and wished Bozo a happy life. Gosh, if I could be a fly on the wall when the crate arrived at the New MFAA! Those nefarious scoundrels, as we nicknamed them, would really get an eye full.

Arizona caused a problem, but we had to work around it. Mostly, I focused on contacting other European museums from the time period, if they were still in existence. Most were either closed or too new to have any reasonable Intel for us. Finally, we got a break toward the end of the fourth day of our week.

Miss Walsh called us together for a meeting without the smallest hint as to what she found. I didn't know it at the time, but her Intel was going to be ground-breaking. Personally, I was affected a lot by its very nature—no doubt there had to be some divine intervention here. I was a believer.

She was strangely quiet. We sat in silence as we watched her organize her paperwork. It seemed like a lot to me. What kind of news could produce this kind of paper trail, all within the last four days? Whatever it was, our time was running dangerously short. When the Wilhelms opened their crate, you-know-what would hit the fan.

"Thank you for being patient with me, kiddos. These past four days have been a test of the human spirit and condition. Many people have given up their privacy and possible safety for us." We sat still and took in what she said. Our eyes never blinked. "So, here it is. I believe, with all my heart, that we've found the true heir to the Van Gogh painting." We all gasped quietly. Jonas began to cry. I think we all did.

"Miss Walsh, please tell us everything. We're ready, aren't we, gang?" Spooky spoke quietly as he represented the club. Miss Walsh smiled back at Spooky. They shared a special bond.

"The folks at the Bode Museum are a close-knit group. They've stayed in touch with those who worked before them, some back as far as World War II if they were still alive. There exists a woman who is still alive. Her name is Anita Boles. She's ninety-one years old. She remembers the Rosens." We all sat up in our chairs and waited for the other shoe to drop.

"She was sixteen at the time, which was approximately 1941. Anita worked as an assistant for filing, typing, and greeting museum goers. She says what she remembers most about the Rosens was their seven-year-olds daughter, Ella."

We all jumped up at once and cheered. We didn't know why because, for all we knew, Ella died along with her parents, but somehow, we felt something awesome was about to happen.

"So sorry, Miss Walsh. We were out of control. Can you please tell us the rest?" Tula put her hands together as if to pray for the story to unfold. Miss Walsh smiled.

"The Rosens went to the museum to see their Van Gogh painting, which hung on the wall in the main room. It had been stolen from them a few weeks earlier by Hitler's Nazis, who then hung it in the museum as a cover. They could simply steal it when they were ready. Anita recalls seven-year-old Ella because they talked a lot when the Rosens visited the museum. They came every Saturday to sit with their painting. Ella, it seemed, confided in Anita that she was scared that something bad was going to happen."

Miss Walsh stopped to wipe tears from her face.

Spooky walked over and consoled her as she had done for him after protective custody.

"Miss Walsh, we've got you. We've got you." He knelt down and hugged her. We all joined around her so that she could calm herself. "Are you okay?" She nodded at us and smiled.

"Yes, thank you. A few nights after Ella's secret talk with Anita, Ella was taken from the Rosens by a neighbor and secretly driven to the Swiss border. They sat in the neighbor's car in the snow, awaiting Ella's pick up. Finally, the Rosens' best friends, who lived in Switzerland, took her with them. They subsequently raised her and never returned to Germany. The following week, the Rosens didn't show up at the museum.

Two days after their daughter was sent to Switzerland, the Nazis took the Rosens to a concentration camp. That was the last time they were seen alive."

We all lowered our heads in prayer for the Rosens, then we looked up at the same time and all asked together. "What happened to Ella?"

"Ella passed away last year. She left a son, Marcus, a grandson, Thaddeus, and a great-granddaughter, Eve Weber, who's thirteen. Eve is your heir to 'The Painter on His Way to Work.' Miss Walsh smiled and raised her hands in celebration. "We've done it, children! This is cause for celebration!"

We celebrated that evening with the parents of the club members. Mr. Heinz returned to Flagstaff to help organize the continuing plan. We had all the correct information but hadn't contacted any family member. Mr. Heinz said we might have to contact the Rosens' best friends, who originally rescued their daughter, Ella. He was confident that, with a little effort, we would succeed in crossing all the T's, as he put it.

At the end of our party that evening, Mr. Heinz excused himself out of the room to accept a long-distance call. I was curious who would call at that hour. I tried my hardest to eavesdrop, but unless I had bionic ears, I wasn't going to get any details. I saw him call Dad and Grandpa into the den with him and Miss Walsh. They were in there for some time. Dad and Grandpa invited Spooky's father into their meeting, too. It dawned on me then that there could be a security issue. Oh boy. Finally, the meeting was over. Mr. Heinz came out first, followed by the others. They all looked serious.

"May I have everyone's attention, please? We need to address a serious situation before the end of this evening." He waited for all of us to gather in a circle, club members up front.

"Dad," I whispered quietly, "What's going on?" I was freaking out a little.

"Trouble, son. We've got some trouble." He looked into my eyes, and I could see worry. Okay, now I was freaking out *a lot*. Mr. Heinz began.

"I'll keep this brief and to the point. The Wilhelms' package arrived two days early. We're not yet sure how that happened as the shipping order was *very* specific about the date of delivery, but nonetheless, they received the crate and have opened it." We all seemed to exclaim words like, *oh no*, and other more grown-up words. "Needless to say, they're on to us in a bigger way than I figured. Apparently, there was an announcement in the Arizona newspapers regarding the reopening of the Lava River Cave since it was re-surveyed after the club found the secret room. Of course, the articles didn't mention what was found in the secret new cave room, but I think they're smart enough to add everything together along with their own suspicions."

Oh boy. We were in *deep* trouble. Dad looked at me with one of the more worried looks I can remember in a long while. Mom was holding Dad's arm tightly. Delilah had a firm grip on my hand. This was all bad news, and we were all scared.

"I can tell you what the Wilhelms know, what I believe they *may* know, and what they probably *do not* know. They know the name of your club. They know Senator Jordan is closely associated. They know the where and when but not about the painting being found in the cave.

It doesn't mean they don't suspect. They never knew where and how the painting was found because I told them the finders wished to remain anonymous. We can assume it's possible they may piece it all together. Folks, we're all in danger, grave danger."

The gang and I huddled in my room for a while to talk. Meanwhile, the parents huddled in the living room, settling on security for each household. My father made a few calls, and it was done. Security was set to follow each of us kids as well as adding to Senator Jordan's detail. After speaking with his service and the reps who kept close eyes on Spooky's family, there was doubt that the Senator wasn't important enough to bother with. Of course, he was a senator, and he *was important*! That would draw obvious attention, and these nefarious scoundrels wanted to blend in with their surroundings.

My club members were smart people. I know I have said this repeatedly. We knew each other better than most others do. We trusted without hesitation, and we planned, *always*, for survival. When Mr. Heinz mentioned Lava River Cave, at first, I had my doubts that the Wilhelms would put two and two together. They would have to have a reason and so far, we weren't aware of one.

We got approval from our folks and from our new security to take a run to Lava River Cave. We wanted to see what changes were made as well as for sentimental reasons. You know how that is. I described how difficult it was for the gang to leave the cave a few months back thinking we wouldn't return.

CHAPTER TWENTY

Meanwhile, somewhere in Belgium, in a warehouse office called New MFAA, Restoring Art to Heirs, the Wilhelms were planning. They had to know the art existed. How? They might have known that all seven of the missing pieces of art and paperwork from the Bode Museum were taken together by professional burglars, the masterly heist. Somewhere in the Wilhelms' past, their grandfather might have helped pull off the art heist and put it safely into the hands of those who would conceal it in secret hiding. At some point, perhaps many years afterward, the art could be retrieved from the hiding place. According to Mr. Heinz the warehouse building the Wilhelms did business in was bugged by European Intelligence. They had a stake in possibly uncovering criminal activity that was decades old. I was happy they were bugged.

"Hilda, where's Duke, for heaven's sake!" Artie Wilhelm seemed impatient as he stared at the painting of Bozo the Clown. It seemed to be mocking him. "Hilda!"

"Yes, yes, Artie, here are the latest files we retrieved yesterday. I was keeping them in the vault. Oh, look," Hilda said, peering from the office window, "there's Duke now." Her German accent was still heavy, but over time she learned to mask it to sound more like Dutch.

"Ah, these files are in remarkable condition, Hilda. Excellent job." The warehouse door flung open as Duke wasted no time joining his cohorts.

"What's up?" Duke was a bit of a dork and not a very polished ringleader. "So, these are the infamous files my grandfather left? Geez, they look like they were created last week. Marvelous! Okay, let me glance at these for a few minutes to see if I can decipher grandpa's chicken scratch."

The three stood together piecing instructions and locations of the first set of files. The instructions were a sort of key, like a treasure map, in a way. They couldn't move to the next until the first key was solved. There was one for each of the missing pieces of original art. How clever of them.

"Well," Duke exclaimed, "we're definitely looking in the correct general area. The latitude and longitude lines put us reasonably close to the U.S. Grand Canyon. What do you think, Artie?"

"If we can somehow connect the random pieces of Intel we have to the locale, we may be on to something. First, why would a state senator's name come up and, second, what does the group called the Young Climbers Club have to do with the senator?

There are also Intel references via an Arizona newspaper about a place called, uh, wait let me find the notes on it." He shuffled through his mountain of notes. "Ah, yes, here it is. Lava River Cave?"

Artie scratched his head for a minute. "Hilda, why don't you open a bottle of wine and put out some snacks. We're going to be at this conversion table most of the night."

Hilda nodded as the three made their plans. Artie walked over to the dart board and pulled a dart from the cork. He slowly walked back toward the Bozo painting.

"Hey, Artie," Duke asked, "what are you doing?" Artie expertly slammed the dart into Bozo's face.

"What I've wanted to do since I opened that stupid crate yesterday." He smiled. "Just a little target practice, my friend. Practice makes perfect." The three thieves laughed loudly.

CHAPTER TWENTY - ONE

At approximately six o'clock the following morning, the alert sirens began ringing at Grandpa's compound. A fire warning rang for the newly arrived Hot Shot crews. They had less than five minutes to dress, grab their gear, and head to the helicopter pad. Grandpa had poured the pad when the barn was converted into fire crew housing. The landing pad had to pass inspection by the U.S. Fire and Safety Division, as well as FAA helicopter guidelines. One crew of twenty ran to the pad. They could hear the whomping sound of the copter blades in the distance. The sun hadn't risen yet, but Grandpa had the place lit up like an airfield.

Each crew member had their talkies tuned to the advanced channel and tested them before boarding the copter for briefing and instruction. Nana said it was a beautiful sight as the copter rapidly went airborne and banked toward the waiting fire. I wish I'd been there.

Meanwhile, back at my house, I woke up hearing Mom

and Dad whispering in the hallway. I looked out the window, and the sun was rising. They were talking about the blaze, its location, and its size. Dad was asked to accompany the lead pilot to help navigate through the heavy smoke. That terrain was tricky, and my father knew it like the back of his hand. His assistance would surely help save lives. Dad had the ability to remain calm in the most stressful situations. That was when his focus was at its peak.

"Dad, where is the burn located?" I was worried because we had so many friends and family scattered around the canyon area.

"It's up in Marble Canyon, son. It's spreading dangerously close to Uncle Danny and Aunt Deb's cabin." Dad looked worried. He and Uncle Danny were close brothers.

"Oh, Dad, I'm so sorry. What can I do? What can the club do?" There had to be something.

Dad thought for a minute.

"Well, kiddo, it all depends on how the fire burns and who will have to be evacuated. I know you and the club have had a lot of experience with evacs, and your time and efforts have been, well, frankly, invaluable. Your training kicks in, and you make a large part of the rescue successful. So, it's a wait-and-see situation. I'll keep you tuned in on a special channel set up at my base box on the table." Holy cow, my father made me feel like a million bucks! I didn't realize that our club's efforts mattered so much.

"You mean I can use your call and pass code to get to you from there?" Dad smiled and nodded. "You can trust me with this, Dad.

"I never doubted you for a moment. I'll keep you up on the latest and the greatest. And good luck with any updates on the painting. Be safe and stay with your bodyguard." Dad was a great dude. "I love you, Deano."

"I love you more." I winked at his way as he swiftly ran out the front door. Phew, this was rough stuff. Of course, I had to update the gang. Tula was taking her Mummo to the airport. She said that her grandma thought her bodyguard was cute. *Brother.* I just shook my head. Spooky had a small competition locally, and Jonas just finished his early yoga class. Jonas would say, *go ahead and laugh at my yoga, but I am the master of controlling my center.* I usually rolled my eyes or nodded repeatedly.

Later that day, according to European Intel, a jet taxied down the runway at Brussels Airport in Belgium. The flight was bound for Las Vegas, Nevada. Again, European Intel had bugged their suspect. Sitting aboard this particular flight was Duke Devlin, grandson of infamous Nazi crook, Heinrich Devlin. Duke and his cohorts, Artie and Hilda Wilhelm, completed converting and deciphering the key needed to release the first bit of information.

That information and the Intel they received were enough to send Duke to the United States.

Before shutting down his cell phone, he touched base with his comrades one last time, "Artie, I'll be on my way in a few minutes. So, we're in agreement with all of our secret code words and Intel email account?" He listened as Artie and Hilda confirmed his request. "All right then. I'll touch base from the New World. I'll let you know when I land. What's that, Artie?" He giggled like an overgrown child. "Ah, Artie, you know me well. I do love a good road trip. Flagstaff or bust!" As he powered down his cell phone, he muttered to himself,

"Get ready, Arizona. Here I come."

Duke Devlin's plane landed at the International Airport in Las Vegas, where he rented an average car, one that wouldn't stand out in a parking lot, and started his road trip to Arizona. He didn't waste any time calling his nefarious cohorts.

"Good morning! It's a sunny day here in downtown Las Vegas. I've never seen so many casinos in one block. How are things going with your Intel, Artie?" Duke awaited an update and any further orders.

"Great! I'm glad you arrived well and are already headed to Arizona. What's your expected arrival time in the Flagstaff area, Duke?" Artie and Wilda were trying to get their time zones in sync. Nine hours was a lot to have to work around.

"Oh, with stops, probably four hours or so. The countryside is pretty here. I might enjoy my road trip." He smiled as he gazed out the window at the mountains in the distance.

"Well, that's all well and good, Duke, but don't forget our agenda. I have a few updates that may prove to help you out greatly." Duke pulled to the side of the road so that he could write some notes on the updates.

"Okay, I want you to always keep the Lava River Cave in the front of your mind. The Young Climbers Club was shown in a newspaper article a few weeks back at that location. I want to know if they have a personal connection, Duke. Also, I have Intel on Senator Jordan of Arizona. He's the father of one of the club members, Bartholomew Jordan. Again, I'm not sure what the connection means, but the more we know, the better. Got all the notes down, Duke?" Artie was anxious about his partner's ability to keep up with his updates.

"Yes, got it all. I'll be in touch when I get closer to

Flagstaff. By the way, did the article mention what the big deal was?" Duke was more curious than ever. His dislike of children was no secret to most who knew him.

"It did. Lava River Cave was celebrating the reopening of the cave due to an addition and restoration."

"Oh, okay. That doesn't sound like much. I'm heading down the highway and will be in touch shortly. I'm looking forward to the mission." He chuckled lightly as he hung up.

CHAPTER TWENTY-TWO

"Mandel Base One, this is auxiliary one. Come in. Mandel Base One, come back."

I'd been lying on my bed, staring at the ceiling since we'd finished supper. I hadn't heard a peep from Dad all day. Finally, I heard him coming in at his base station. I sprang about five feet above the bed and ran down the hall as fast as I could. Suddenly, I wiped out in the middle of the hallway as the hall runner became my magic carpet. I came to a stop directly in front of the table that held Dad's base box.

"This is Base One. You're coming in loud and clear, auxiliary one. How are you, Dad? Come back." I was never so glad to hear Dad's voice.

"How are things, Dean? Any 'word' on the Van Gogh episode? Over."

" Miss Walsh and Mr. Heinz are coming back tomorrow morning. They have definite news, and we'll probably be able to move forward with locating the Rosens' lost heir, Eve

Weber." I was still worried about Uncle Danny and Aunt Deb. "Dad, how is Uncle Danny?"

"We've been praying for their safety. Over."

"Well, that's why I reached out to you. We've got them, and I'm sending them to your grandparents for a few days until the area is safe to return to. The blaze is a little close to their cabin, and the conditions are too dangerous to remain with their friends. They're already airborne and expected on the copter pad in about half an hour. Over."

"That's awesome news, Dad! I'll wait till tomorrow to race over for a visit. When are you coming back? Is the fire under control? Over."

"If the conditions remain calm and damp, we have a chance to get this under control by daybreak: no casualties and only minor injuries. I'll keep you all informed. Gotta run, kiddo.

Hugs for you and Delilah, you hear. Over."

"Yes, sir! Back to you and be safe. Out"

Good grief, what a relief to hear from Dad that my aunt and uncle were safe. With the fire season starting out like this, it could be a long and hard summer.

CHAPTER TWENTY-THREE

Mr. Heinz and Miss Walsh arrived earlier that morning after I'd spent a little time with Uncle Danny. It was good to see them, and I was glad they were safe. Nana had planned a family supper for later, so we'd all have a chance to catch up and enjoy the visit. Dad was heading back to the base and would grab a jeep and drive home later that afternoon.

The gang gathered at my house while Mr. Heinz and Miss Walsh prepared to begin their meeting. He asked some of the parents to attend as well. We had enough parents present, along with our bodyguards, so we began the meeting. It was hard to read their faces. Whenever we were having a meeting involving new information, Mr. Heinz looked emotionless and focused. Today was no different.

"Straight to it, folks." Mr. Heinz sighed. "As you know from Intel coming in, we have discovered a new partner associated with the two Wilhelm grandchildren. His name is Duke Devlin. His grandfather was notorious Nazi badman, Heinrich Devlin.

According to European Intel, we're reasonably sure Heinrich Devlin led the art heist at the Bode Museum as the war was ending. Mr. Devlin appears to be our ringleader." He looked over the rim of his glasses and forced a smile. "So, is everyone okay so far?"

I jumped right in with a question in the silence of my living room.

"So, this Duke fellow not only knows the Wilhelms, but their grandparents worked together to pull off this monster heist? After all these years, how do they know what to do, and where are they *possibly* getting their Intel after decades? Was it, like, willed to them?" I felt stupid for asking that question, but nothing else would've made sense. Miss Walsh stepped forward.

"Well, Dean, in a way, you're correct, but not in the traditional sense." She looked at Mr. Heinz. He nodded for her to continue.

"While Heinrich Devlin wasn't a direct confidant to Hitler, he worked closely with Hans Wilhelm in his efforts to push Hitler toward more control over larger areas. We know, of course, this didn't come to fruition, but Heinrich and Hans convinced Hitler that continuing to compile immense wealth would keep his cause moving forward for generations. Thus, the bi-time art heist." She always made perfect sense.

"That does make sense, but how are Duke and his cohorts able to know this information and process it in *the present* day? I mean, geez, they'd almost have to have a treasure map!" I said that sarcastically but didn't expect their response. Miss Walsh and Mr. Heinz looked at each other after my comment. "Oh, you're not serious?" I was shocked that my idiotic guess was even close.

"As a matter of fact," Mr. Heinz responded, "you're right on point." Everyone stopped and whispered in disbelief. "We haven't put all the pieces together, but it's been reported that it won't take long, thanks to today's computer programs. Europe's FBI can go where we can't even fathom." Spooky chimed in as he understood groups such as that with a major politician for a father.

"Yep, that's a fact. I can't even imagine what they see. I'm sure it would curl our toes, as my Mom would say." Everyone giggled.

"So, what are those feds suggesting, Mr. Heinz?"

"Well, Spooky, they believe that the means available to spies and major crime rings then are being used now. For one, encryption. We use it even today, but remember, they had no computer means. Coding and encryption were reasonably effective and still used today when one wants to duck from cyberspace." He cleared his throat. "Intel believes that the location of files for the seven pieces of art that were stolen lies with the Wilhelms and that they've begun the process. They know at least one piece of art has surfaced. Intel suggests they have a pretty good idea where to look." He swallowed hard. I had a sinking feeling in the pit of my stomach. I looked at Grandpa. He was strangely quiet. After an eerie length of silence, Jonas spoke up.

"Well, I'm sure I'm not the only one thinking this right now, but what is the worst thing you're going to tell us? This has surely been a build-up. Please tell us." He waited for a moment as our two confidants stared out into the room. Everyone was waiting for the bomb.

"They'll surely be coming to Arizona if they haven't

arrived already. It may be one or all three of them. They may have thugs for support, or they may use them from a U.S. source. They'll blend—no fancy clothes or cars.

If Duke Devlin is as savvy with encryption and decoding as Intel suggests, they've successfully unlocked their first step of encoding. Likely, they may have had the aid of something as simple as Earth's meridians and as complicated as conversion tables."

Mr. Heinz went into further detail about everyday activities like our summer competitions. He insisted we go and have our bodyguards close. They could blend in as an old Uncle Norman or an assistant to a coach. Heinz was insistent that we do not blink. We must act totally 'normal and unaware' that anything criminal may be within our reach. Easier said than done.

Miss Walsh adjourned our meeting by saying the criminals had covered their bases well. They truly were masterminds. After all, ghosts couldn't tell people seventy years later where they hid the art, now could they? This was almost too big to wrap my brain around, yet we all seemed to be present with the plan. I looked around for Grandpa, but he'd disappeared. That was weird.

CHAPTER TWENTY-FOUR

As afternoon came around, Dad's copter finally reached the Camp Navajo Army Base on the outskirts of town. Because of his high rank with the Night Stalkers, he was permitted to sign out pretty much anything he needed from the base. He signed out a jeep and would have it picked up at our house by someone from the base later that afternoon.

Dad decided to stop at the Shell station in town for a large coffee. He was unaware that Duke Devlin was pumping gas only yards across the parking lot. Even though Dad knew who Duke Devlin was, Dad didn't know what Duke looked like. Duke wouldn't have known who Dad was or what he looked like either.

As Dad walked up to the register to pay for his coffee and snacks, he stood behind a large, burly man with an accent. It was Duke. Dad didn't pay much attention except that ringing up the gas he'd pumped seemed to take a long time. The attendant was having computer troubles. Finally, he succeeded in ringing up Duke's gas transaction. As he turned, he almost ran square into my father. Their eyes met, but Duke was quick to smile and utter an apology.

"No problem," Dad replied.

They literally 'brushed arms,' yet they were clueless about who each other was. Funny things like this happen all the time. Mom called it happenstance. She says it was something that was meant to happen by accident. Cosmic. I didn't do cosmic very well. You could ask Vincent Van Gogh.

By the time Dad got home, we briefed him in detail about the afternoon's busy meeting. He wasn't surprised. Our Intel predicted they would soon travel. He definitely wasn't surprised because they must have been really mad when they opened their crate and saw Bozo, the clown staring at them! I also took the time to get all the grizzly details about the blaze. The bottom line was that the Hot Shot crews and Fire Jumpers did a remarkable job. Dad was more than pleased.

"I wish you could have seen this year's crew, son. They were amazing and fearless, but safety was always number one. Which reminds me, did you see Uncle Danny and Aunt Deb?"

"Aunt Deb was extremely worried about their home and their friends who lived nearby them. It all made her cry, and I can't say I blame her. Uncle Danny was, well, you know, cool. What's your saying? He marches to the beat of a different drum?" We both laughed. We loved him any way he was. "I told him we'd all chill at Nana Sarah's dinner tonight."

The dinner at my grandparents was strictly a family evening: no art dealers, no club members. We hadn't had a good family night in a long time. The only others in and around the house were bodyguards. Everyone chipped in with their best dish, and we ended with BBQ ribs and chicken, fire-roasted baked potatoes, and a Caesar salad. Mom made a big tray of pear/apple crisp to top it all off. By the end of dinner, we were full and content. Somehow, we made our way to the living room couch and plopped like righteously stuffed folks do.

I happened to glance across the room and saw Grandpa hanging around the kitchen counter. He looked strange, sort of like he was up to something secretive. I looked over again and could have sworn he was talking to his wristwatch! I must have imagined it, and then he did it again. I was curious and walked over to see if he was okay.

"Grandpa, what'cha doing over here by yourself?" He looked nonchalant.

"Oh, just digesting my food. I like standing for a while after I eat. I also had a buddy call from the Moose Club. That and I was listening to the final baseball scores through my earbuds." He seemed satisfied with his explanation.

"Huh, well, that's good because if you want to hear something funny, I thought you were talking to your wristwatch! That's a riot, isn't it?" We both laughed.

"Well, I'll excuse myself for a few minutes to check on the returning crews. See you in a few."

I turned to walk back to the couch and noticed his cell phone on the kitchen counter across the room. How could he have taken a cell phone call or listened to scores? I was worried.

I wondered whether I should tell Dad about this. I decided not to but to keep my eye on him. Before I got back to the couch, there was an urgent knock at the front door. The guard opened the door. It was Mr. Heinz. He looked absolutely frantic but tried to keep his cool. Just then, Grandpa walked in the back door. He saw Mr. Heinz and stopped in his tracks.

"Ernie?"

"Rosie, they're here." The air in the room seemed to stop. "Duke Devlin arrived in Flagstaff earlier and checked into a local motel. I want the senator's Detail beefed up, as well as these guards. Notify the gang's parents." Heinz stopped for a minute to collect his thoughts.

"The Van Gogh." Grandpa realized it was below us in his room-sized safe. "I'm calling the security company and putting them on alert. Time to double up on the codes."

"So, everyone, the time has come quicker than we expected. Duke Devlin is not only on U.S. soil, but in our town. Rosie, you know what to do." Grandpa nodded knowingly at Mr. Heinz. I was clueless. I had no idea what was happening except that some bad dudes were a few miles from our house.

According to European Intel, Duke Devlin's bug picked up a call to his cohorts from the comfort of his Days Inn motel room. More Intel flooded in. He wrote feverishly as Artie continued to update Duke on the latest. They knew who we were and where we lived, and they were coming for the painting. If they couldn't get to the painting, they would surely come for us.

I didn't know how I would pull it off, but I wanted my club members with me right away. I felt responsible for them and said so out loud in a room full of people.

At this point, the room was spinning. I was totally freaking out! That night, the entire room of people at Grandpa's house ran to my side.

Uncle Danny and Aunt Deb were an unexpected source of

comfort. They knew me well and how to calm me. Everyone in the room knew me well.

Finally, after several minutes of totally freaking out and scaring Mom half to death, the room stopped spinning, and I felt like I was calming down. I questioned whether Mom slipped me something, but she swears she didn't.

My parents sat with me on the couch. Mom took my hand and winked at me while Dad leaned in for a quiet talk.

"Dean, your mother and I have supported you and the club because we know how responsible and capable you are. We raised you to be a conscientious young man with very deep values and character. We're proud of you and in awe of the young man you've become. We're humbled and wish others had sons in their lives like you." I smiled and shook my head.

Jonas was sitting on the arm of the sofa within earshot. I saw a tear run down his cheek, that mush ball.

"Wow, you two. I feel I owe it all to you and your great sense of honesty, integrity, and direction. I'm a product of 'you'." Mom and Dad smiled at each other, then focused back on our heavy conversation.

"When we and the other parents first heard the news from Ernie Heinz that the folks who misrepresented themselves were the bad guys, we all went into protection mode. It's not a slight against your club's good judgment. This is purely parent/child related. It's our job as your parents to protect you no matter what, come what may," Dad said.

"Agreed, and I totally understand. So, what did you and the other parents come up with?"

"Well, after our brainstorm of introducing the Bozo

painting, we were at a loss. Then we realized it was time to call in some reinforcements." I was puzzled by what he meant. "Reinforcements?" I asked, and Dad smiled.

CHAPTER TWENTY-SIX

"Do you remember the Coconino National Authority investigator? His name is Zach Duvall, along with his deputy, Nate Brown?" Dad said. I nodded as I recalled that day vividly. "That was some day, wasn't it, son? They'll have a role in this strategy and are working with Lava River Cave to help with our plan. This way, you won't be too surprised to see them, but I can't tell you where and when you will." Oh, brother, this reminded me of an old Hardy Boys mystery, but *much* cooler.

Mr. Duvall sort of 'grew on me.' I loved the look on his face when the rock door rumbled, and the door to the secret room opened! What a hoot! We both got a good chuckle.

"Also, a few buddies of mine from the Night Stalkers, off -of course, are involved," Dad said. "It's they who have offered objective help and clarity in suggesting a goal. We needed to begin something official with the folks at Lava River Cave by going back to Coconino Forestry for guidance. They willingly agreed. Dean, there is a plan, but I can't tell you what it is. We can only guide you and the club on what to do. Do we understand each other?"

"Oh, yes, and we're all relieved to hear this! We may be responsible and capable, but we *are* still kids." I thought for a minute. "Do the bodyguards know a few Stalkers are involved? Where are they? Are they going to be an active part of unfolding your plan?" Dad laughed at my battery of questions.

"Yes. Closer than you think. And yes." Dad looked at me with the Cheshire grin I swear he stole from Spooky. I knew even if I began guessing where the Night Stalkers were, he would neither confirm nor deny, so I knew I was on my own. "Dean, in the general scheme of things, it's probably less important to know where they are. Just know that they'll have your back and focus on performing the tasks asked of you and the club. We believe in you all the way."

CHAPTER TWENTY-SEVEN

Mom, Dad, Delilah, and I all stayed the night at Grandpa's in a couple of his many guest quarters. We'd planned to stay and visit with Andy and Deb anyway. I'd texted the gang the night before after my long talk with the folks. I explained it all. What their parents hadn't told them, I filled in the blanks. They were as happy as I was and felt relieved because we now felt safe and free to do what we set out to do. Our goal had always been to put that beautiful Vincent Van Gogh painting with its rightful and deserving heir. Now, we were close to realizing our dream. I envisioned it would be a wonderful, rewarding day.

The morning was warm for early June. I hit the pool for fifteen minutes of laps. I felt a splash as I dashed by the center of the pool, only to see Delilah doing the backstroke. She was wearing a big grin. Delilah was probably one of the most advanced swimmers for a seven-year-old I'd seen.

She was like a fish and felt perfectly at home in the water. What she loved most of all was floating. No drooping legs, no saggy bottom, all float; she could do it for hours if Mom let her. This was just what I needed. I felt rejuvenated and ready to face our day.

The gang was due to arrive any minute. Although I didn't look out the front of the property, I was told it was likely the properties were all being watched by the thugs Duke Devlin hired. I counted three bodyguards dressed as family swimmers around the pool, one lady and two men. I wasn't especially worried. I remember Mr. Heinz telling us the bad dudes wanted to blend and wouldn't create a scene unless it was imminent.

I came through the back door into the kitchen as I dried my pool trunks. I looked out the front window and saw a rug and drapery cleaning truck pull up. I felt a little uneasy as I heard a knock at the door. Nana answered.

"Good morning, Mrs. Mandel. I have your order clean and ready." She pulled out an order sheet and read Nana's bill.

"Let's see, two area rugs and a four-panel set of cranberry drapes?"

"Yes," Nana replied. "You may bring the items right through the front door."

I watched as the lady and her associate stepped into the back of the cleaning truck to get Nana's order. Each lady stepped off the truck, holding rugs and drapes in the air and over their heads so they didn't drag. They walked side by side to the door.

"Oh, they look lovely. Won't you step in with the items?" Nana seemed pleased.

When I heard the front door close, the delivery ladies slowly stepped aside to reveal my three wayward club members.

They had simply walked unseen across the driveway in the middle of the garments! This was a first, even for us. *Fantastic!*

The gang and I chatted it up for a few minutes, and when we turned around to thank the ladies from the drapery truck, they were gone. They quietly slipped out. I suppose it was meant to look like any other dry-clean delivery. My club retired to the vault room downstairs so that we could be with the painting. It reminded us just how important it was to get through this plan and into the business of getting the Van Gogh to Eve Weber.

One thing we discussed was the status of connecting to Eve Weber and her family.

Miss Walsh kept us up to date. According to her, things were moving together well. We expected daily updates at this point because we were that close. Now, all we had to do was protect the painting and stay alive. Oh, brother.

The Wilhelms had traveled to the United States to join their partner in crime, Duke Devlin. They'd been bugged the same way Devlin had. According to Intel, they'd already landed in Vegas en route to Flagstaff, not far from its outskirts. That thought made my stomach do flip-flops.

To be safe, they arranged to meet at an abandoned service station on the edge of town. The three criminals were lying as low as they could. Because the authorities had numerous photos of them, they didn't take any chances and avoided stupid mistakes. They dressed the part with disguises so that they would blend.

Miss Walsh said her intel confirmed that the gang planned to split up for the time being. Hilda agreed to go with Duke and pose as his wife. Artie used his old man get-up and some convincing make-up. Between them, you never would've known they were nefarious scoundrels. I still loved that word.

The gang and I had been down in the vault room for a few hours talking about how we thought the ceremony with Eve Weber would go. We could envision handing the painting over to her with tremendous gratitude. *Well, shucks, it was really nothing at all.*

"Hey, you know my stomach is growling. What time is it?" Tula had a limitless pit. It was one o'clock, though. We were all hungry.

"It's lunchtime, that's what, and I've got a tidbit to share," Tula said.

Jonas was curious. "Do tell, please share. And it better be tasty."

Everyone laughed because they loved Jonas' silly antics.

"Last night, Nana Sarah made *I-talian* meatballs, and we had a meatball-palooza!"

Everyone cheered. Suddenly, I was the keeper of the key to paradise. "Oh, yeah, and there are lots of them in there."

Spooky couldn't resist the tagline I left for him. "Dude, you mean you didn't finish them off? I thought I raised you better." We all laughed as we reached the main floor landing off the kitchen.

"Hey, got any of her crispy rolls left and *cheese, please*!" Tula snorted.

"Spooky, you're such a hog. I'll let you borrow the cheese after I consume mass quantities."

While Tula and Spooky bantered, Jonas whispered a few thoughts to me.

"Hey, Deano, so you feel pretty confident that the big guns are taking care of the scary stuff?"

"Oh, Jonas, I was thinking there's a good chance it'll be over before we know it. They probably wouldn't need us anyway. I think my Dad wanted to cover his bases, which is good, so yeah, not to worry, Cuz. It's all good. Trust me." By then, the meatballs were reheated, and the gang and I sat at the counter and began consuming the meatball sandwiches. Yup, no doubt they were the bomb.

"Hey, you! Down there!" Tula leaned across the counter and grinned at Spooky. "Keeper of the cheese. May I please partake in a peasant's portion? Promise I'll give it back, *dork!*"

We all had to put our sandwiches down because we couldn't control our laughter. "Cheese, please, Mr. *Cheesehead.*" Tula was ribbing Spooky pretty well. "And, *furthermore*, you'd better hand it over!"

CHAPTER TWENTY-SEVEN

Suddenly, the Hot Shot fire alarm began firing its timely beeps loudly. We all froze for a minute because we didn't expect it would go off. Quite frankly, what with everything else, I totally forgot the crews were out there. I jumped down from my stool and walked slowly to the back window, watching activity from the crew's quarters.

"The crews have five minutes to take care of business and grab their gear." I stopped for a minute to listen to the approaching copter. The thumping echo of the blades tipped me off. "There are two copters, which means both crews are going. It must be a bad burn. Hurry, let's go downstairs and watch."

We ran quickly down the back stairs to the exit door where the crews came out. A few crew members were already waiting on the pad. Tula and Jonas were the only two who had never been on rescue as Spook and I had, but they'd been involved in other important ways. Their eyes were fixed on the sky as the copters came into view.

I counted them out as they ran to the pad. *Seven, eight, nine*, "Hey wait a minute. I only see one crew. I wonder if the other crew is waiting till the other copter leaves," Spooky agreed.

"Yeah, dude, that's probably it. *Whoa!*" Before we realized what was happening, the four of us were being dragged quickly by the arm toward the second copter. We looked over and saw they were our bodyguards. They never looked at us and didn't slow their fast pace. We were lifted swiftly into the waiting copter without any resistance. We knew it had something to do with the plan to capture the art thieves.

We were met by two serious, muscular looking guys. At first, I thought it *was* the bad guys, but knew if our bodyguards had deposited us on the copter, they couldn't be.

The man on the left put his index finger up to his lips indicating he wanted quiet. The other was watching the copter pilot. I knew many of them, but I didn't recognize him.

Finally, the copter pilot gave his thumbs up to the two men. "A-okay. You're good to go for two minutes." They looked at us and one of them spoke.

"Hello, kids. We're friends of your dad's." We were relieved because I knew it had to be Dad's two buddies from the Night Stalkers. "My name is Jack, and this is Tom. We're not here on official business, understood?" We nodded back to them.

"But you're here to help us and help protect the Van Gogh, right?" I said. He smiled back at me and nodded.

"I have a temporary communications silencer on this rig for our safety, so I'll be brief. Listen well. We get one shot at this, understood?" Again, we nodded.

"Okay, we'll drop you in the field behind the old Wrigley Chewing Gum billboard. There, you'll see backpacks to assist you and bikes to get you quickly to the entrance to Lava River Cave. You're to ditch your bikes at the back side of the cave away from view. Got it so far?" We all nodded. "Take the backpacks and run to the entrance to the cave. You'll be met by two individuals who will give you further instructions. Any questions?" I spoke up quickly.

"Where are the bad guys? I presume you know who I mean."

"Affirmative. We're not sure, but believe they won't be far behind, so it's important that you go quickly and resist preoccupying your focus on where they are."

"How do they know where we are?"

He was quick to answer. "How did we know where *you* were? Intel, except ours is uber better." He winked. "Keep your heads down and follow my instructions. You'll be protected at all times. If you're ready, the temporary silencer will terminate, and our air will be live. After I give you a directive for total silence you're to remain totally silent until you reach your party at the cave entrance. This is *paramount*. Understood?" We nodded once again. "On my mark. Five, four, three," counting the last two with a nod, then, his finger went back to his lips. "Hot Shot stable, this is Hot Shot two, come back."

"We read you stable leader, go ahead."

"We're departing home base pad for assigned burn. ETA fifteen hundred hours. Come back."

"Roger that. Safe journey. Over and out."

By this time, our adrenaline was racing. We sat in silence and stared back at each other. We all realized we were in the thick of it. This was it. It was happening. As we looked down and saw the old familiar billboard coming into view, we put our hands one over the other, in the center of our circle. Jack and Tom laid their hands over ours and smiled at us. We did a silent, *one, two, three, group!* I felt the copter land. Jack nodded to hop out and gave us two thumbs up. We ran toward the billboard in silence and never looked back.

During the few minutes it took to run the tenth of a mile or so from the drop toward the billboard, a thousand things ran through my head. I recalled the night the gang and I called Grandpa from the entrance to Lava River with the Van Gogh painting in our hands. It was nearly ten o'clock that night. We ran all the way to the billboard where we hid with the painting until he arrived. There was the time we took Dad and Grandpa into the cave where they collected debris that was left behind. The thieves' trash turned out to be valuable clues. Finally, the time we met Duvall and took them into the secret room. The look on his face was priceless.

While we peddled quickly toward the cave, I looked at my fellow club members and saw the same look on their face I must have worn. It helped keep us focused and eager to get to the entrance unseen or, worse yet, attacked by nefarious scoundrels.

CHAPTER TWENTY-EIGHT

Keeping our vow of silence, we arrived at the back side of the cave where we ditched the bikes and headed with our backpacks toward the entrance. We scanned the area the best we could but didn't see any signs of other people. The fact that it was still daylight wasn't in our favor. We might not have spotted anyone hiding in the area, but they might have clearly seen our every move. We couldn't worry about that now.

We finally arrived, a little out of breath between the run and the bike ride. There was no sign of anyone there to meet us. I panicked and spun around only to find Inspector Duvall staring at me. Jonas spotted his deputy, Nate Brown, just inside the cave.

"Duvall," I whispered, "what are you doing here?"

"Nate and I are here to see you through the entrance to the cave and update you. We've just been advised that the group of art thieves and their thugs are within one mile. You must go as quickly as you can to the secret room. Don't speak and don't shine any light that you won't need. Try to use these illuminated wrist bands."

"Yeah, but how do we know what to do when we get there?" I was scared and so was the gang.

"The same way you did from your grandfathers to the helicopter and the helicopter to here. Someone will always have your back. You all are incredibly intuitive. Use it! Now, go quietly."

Again, we pushed forward and never looked back. Nate whispered to us to be careful as we passed him with high fives. With one big deep breath we were off on the next leg of our journey. At this point, I had no idea what to expect when we got to what was once the secret room. We knew that the restoration opened the room to the public and saw that for ourselves during the grand re-opening. So, what? We arrived at a dead end, with no place to hide, and fight the bad guys with our flashlights and water bottles? Holy crap! There was no way we were losing this fight!

Just then, I heard a thump and moan from behind me. Jonas went down. He tried to bear the pain of his fall without moaning out loud. He shook his head indicating that he couldn't go. I knelt next to him and whispered in a micro-quiet voice, "Now, you listen to me, Cuz. Get up off your butt and start moving. Our lives depend on it."

He responded also in a low whisper. "But there just isn't enough light. My eyes won't adjust to blackness." I grabbed the sides of his head with my hands and pulled him to me again.

"Then look with your *other* set of eyes." I pulled back and a Jonas-look-of-wonderment came over his face. He nodded with a smile. I motioned to push forward.

We were almost there. It was dark and scary. We arrived at what recently became an open doorway to the secret room. It was sealed just as it had been when we found it during Spring Break. I turned and looked at the others. Tula reached into her sack and pulled out a glove. I realized she was telling me to drop to my belly and feel for the door release lever. I shook my head. I couldn't imagine for a minute that it was there.

The ground was damp and dirty. I'd almost given up, but then, success! Just like old times, the rock rumbled, moved, and revealed the secret room. We were shocked when we cast our eyes inside.

"Grandpa!" I tried to whisper my shout. "What are you doing here?" He smiled a small smile and didn't answer. Grandpa stepped to one side. The oil lamp was turned way down, which gave just enough light to see that the Van Gogh painting was on an easel right behind him.

"Step inside, son." I looked over and saw Dad, Jack and Tom.

How did they get there so fast?

We moved inside enough for the trigger to close the door.

"What's all this, Dad? And why is Grandpa here?"

"Grandpa has been our eyes and ears for all the foreign and domestic Intel." I looked confused.

"But only the CIA can do stuff like that, right?" I looked over at Dad and Grandpa.

Dad answered his father. "Grandpa *is* CIA. It's what he spent much of his adult life doing alongside his fire department duty."

Alrighty, then. I was sure I was going to faint. Grandpa, a secret agent with the CIA? Next thing you'd tell me was that Nana Sarah was a steam ship Captain! I rolled my eyes. Spooky just nodded his head in that *dude* kind of way. "They'll be here momentarily. Step to the far side of the cave, gang." We followed Dad's instruction.

I whispered to him. "Why are *we* here?" He walked over and looked at each of them with admiration.

"Because you *deserve* to be here for this." I was speechless. We all stood together closely and waited.

Jack and Tom took their places on either side of the rock door, ready to pounce onto the bad guys. Grandpa, meanwhile, was talking to his watch again. I *knew* I wasn't imagining it. Now I understand. He was talking with outside sources, delivering a play-by-play update as well as talking to Duvall to verify that the art thieves were on their way through the cave. They knew the painting was there because Dad had staged it so they would know it was for sure.

CHAPTER TWENTY-NINE

The rest happened quickly. Tom and Jack stepped onto the door release as the thieves arrived. After they saw the painting, they went for it, of course, but were swiftly put down by the two unofficial Night Stalkers. For the first time, we saw the faces of Hilda and Artie Wilhelm. Their glance in our direction was *not* nice. Jonas lowered his head and couldn't look at them anymore.

The three thugs they'd brought with them were easily subdued by Inspector Duvall, Deputy Brown, and my father. Local authorities were waiting outside the cave by the dozens. The only one who was missing was Duke Devlin. I asked Duvall about him on our way out of the cave.

"It seems these horrible criminals were smart enough to send one of their most powerful and involved players back to Europe. In lieu of the long, incredible connection to stolen art from almost seventy-five years ago and the implications of connections to Hitler, there's a long line of authorities who want answers and closure. I'd love to be a fly on the wall for this one.

"They still might get Duke, though, right? I mean, he's not just going to wander around causing trouble and threatening people's lives, is he?" Duvall smiled.

"Wandering isn't something Duke will have the pleasure of doing for quite a long time. Only time will tell. For now, your Van Gogh painting is free to be restored. I imagine the exciting day will come before too long when you'll present this history to your newfound heir."

I liked Duvall. He was smart, sensitive, and far more savvy than I ever gave him credit for. When we arrived back in the sunlight outside the cave, I spotted Miss Walsh and Mr. Heinz right away. Boy were they a sight for sore eyes. They both ran toward us.

"Hey, gang, you've done it! The scary part is over; now we can begin cleaning and restoration. It's about time." They carefully retrieved the painting and sat with us in a large, official-looking van. At least, I think it was. There were no markings on it. It was black with dark-tinted windows, and we were closely followed by a security motorcade. Once we got moving, Miss Walsh leaned in with her sweet British grin.

"Alright, children. Let's hear it. The *real* story, and don't leave *one thing out*, now, you hear?"

While Spooky began telling our exciting tale, I leaned in and whispered to my father. "Dad, where's Grandpa?" He told me he was on a private jet to Washington, D.C..

I didn't ask. He didn't tell. We just smiled at each other.

"What a day."

CHAPTER THIRTY

The weeks following the arrests of Hilda and Artie Wilhelm for their part in one of the worst international crime rings were a blur.

Their criminal charges filled an entire sheet of paper: crimes against country, against the innocent victims during WWII, and against humanity. Too much to ponder, said Nana.

I felt both exhausted and exhilarated.

Mostly, I was looking forward to the ceremony of finally passing the Van Gogh painting to Eve Weber and her family.

By now, it was pushing the third week of June. Jonas and I had celebrated our thirteenth birthdays the week before. We went to a rodeo, followed by our serious consumption of the best steak burgers on the planet. You don't know what you're missing if you've never had homemade tater tots.

The whole gang had a blast. It was a way to reconnect to our roots and our club. It was like being *home* again.

The club also planned to install our new club member,

Emily Davis.

I talked about Emily at the beginning of my story. We were as excited as she was but knew the ceremony came first.

It was scheduled for three days from now in Phoenix. It was turning out to be a special, some said historic, ceremony.

I could understand why.

Since the gang and I became affixed to the historic work of the Monuments Men and their contributions during World War II, we understood how important this ceremony was, pomp and circumstance aside.

It represented a triumph over evil, righting a wrong, and drawing attention to this part of history that often is forgotten.

My club now felt permanently connected to this past. We were part of it, and it was part of us.

The celebration would take place at the capitol building in Phoenix, a couple hours south of Flagstaff. The gang and I had spent many days there for important competitions. The ceremony itself would be in the Rotunda of the Capitol.

We were honored to have both Senator Jordan and Senator McCain present along with Governor Ducey. Anita Boles, the lady who knew the Rosens and Eve Weber's great-grandmother, Ella, was to be there. She put all the pieces together, and the gang and I couldn't wait to meet her.

Also attending was to be a representative from the Bode Museum in Germany. Of course, it wouldn't be the same without Mr. Heinz and Miss Walsh. I couldn't imagine where we would've been without them.

Eve Weber, her father, and her grandfather would be there. Eve would accept the painting on behalf of the family.

CHAPTER THIRTY-ONE

Finally, the day of the ceremony arrived. I was nervous and excited. It was still early that morning. I was laying out my new suit. Our parents took the club out shopping the week before for new threads.

The three dudes ended up with black suits and classic white shirts. I loved the super thin black ties that matched. We looked sort of like the Beatles back in the day.

I guess Tula was our fourth Beatle, but she cleaned up way better than we did. She was dressed in an elegant black satin evening gown with a white satin collar and sash. Her mother pulled her ash blonde hair into a twist to the side. Whatever the girls call that hairdo, it looked nice on her.

Dad knocked on my door that morning.

"Wow, Dad, you look great in your penguin suit."

"Not as stylish as you dudes. What did you call these suits? Beatles duds?" He said, checking out my threads. "You look handsome, Dean. Good Lord, you're going to break a lot of hearts."

"Aw shucks, Dad." I looked back at him and noticed a funny look on his face. It was a face not many knew as strange, but it usually meant trouble.

"Dad, is something wrong?" He looked at me with a strange look.

"What do you mean? I'm excited about the day, aren't you?" He was trying hard to evade my question, but I wasn't buying it. I nodded.

"Yep, I'm looking forward to it, too. You didn't answer my question. What are you *not* telling me?" He tried to stare me down, but I didn't flinch. He sighed and sat on the edge of my bed.

"I have an assignment, Dean. I'm leaving tonight." I thought I recognized that look. It was the same look I saw on his face when I was six years old when he left for the Middle East to help take down Usama bin Laden. I didn't ask, and he didn't tell. I knew he couldn't. I sighed and sat next to him.

"So, I guess you can't say anything about anything? How long? One day? One year?" His eyes never left mine. His expression never flinched. The answer was always silence, and I understood it. I wouldn't say I liked it, but I knew what he did and how important it was for the welfare of a lot of people.

"That's okay, Dad." I took his hand. "I understand." We smiled at each other. "So, how about those Diamondbacks?" We both burst out laughing.

CHAPTER THIRTY-TWO

We arrived at the Arizona State Capitol Building by eleven that morning. The day was gorgeous, and the gardens, where the reception would later take place, looked amazing! It was scattered with white chairs and tables, a table where food would later be served, and so many flowers I was almost overwhelmed. The breeze felt gentle and dry. My club and I stood together, alone, taking in the beauty and snapping lots of pictures. Suddenly, a man walked out of the building toward us. We weren't sure who he was, but he was smiling.

"Hello," the man said with broken English, "my name is Thaddeus Weber. I am Eve's papa." We were surprised to see him and thrilled that they had arrived safely. My stomach was filled with butterflies.

We cordially shook his hand. He apparently knew who we were.

"Eve would like to meet you before the ceremony begins. Is this acceptable to you?" He was formal and treated us with a high level of respect. I answered on behalf of the club.

"Yes, yes! We're excited to see her, and it would be our pleasure to meet her now. Here? In the gardens?" Just as I asked my questions, the same door opened where Mr. Weber entered the garden. There she was. Eve Weber. Eve walked directly toward us, smiling with every step she took. By the time she reached us, we were all running toward each other. It was a great group hug. Tears were shed as we quietly continued our embrace. I heard camera shutters clicking in the distance.

We shared a deep, unspoken bond. The closest I came to this experience and feeling was with my own club. It was intense. Finally, she pulled back and looked at each of us, one by one, smiling.

"Thank you from the bottom of my heart. You." She stopped to compose her tears." You are *my* Monuments Kids." We were overwhelmed and in awe of her gratitude. "You've moved through this plan God bestowed upon you with strength and grace. My family offers you our deepest gratitude. More importantly, my Mother Land thanks you." We knew that although Ella didn't live in Germany beyond the age of six or seven, Eve's connection to her great-grandmother would live on through her. Those few moments, for me, trumped anything that could possibly happen for the rest of the ceremony. Although scary at times, every moment of this excellent adventure was worth it, and I have no doubts or regrets.

The ceremony was scheduled for one o'clock on the rotunda floor. We had five minutes to stare at the goings-on, as Nana called it.

I saw an elderly woman sitting in a chair across from us

whom I thought might have been Anita Boles. She looked at us and waved her hand at the gang. We waved and smiled.

There was a banner over the podium that was beautifully handmade. It read *I dream of painting and then paint my dreams.* That was a Van Gogh quote. I remember Jonas sharing quite a few of them. I looked over at Jonas. He was smiling all goo-goo eyed at Eve. I do believe he was smitten. Finally, the ceremony began.

Governor Ducey was introduced and took to the podium. He talked about history, art, culture, and how great it was when we could embrace them and keep them in the forefront of our existence. The governor introduced Senator Jordan. He looked as proud as a peacock as he looked over at the club.

His speech was a bit like the Governor's, but it was much more heartfelt because he had been personally involved with Spooky as his son.

Before the Governor presented the painting to the family, which had been covered on an easel near the podium, he introduced Eve to the microphone. She'd arranged to recite a favorite Van Gogh quote of hers. It was special to her because her great-grandmother recited it to her many times as a young child.

With poise and grace, she took the podium. Eve spoke very good English and annunciated well in front of others. She taught me some excellent pointers before I took the microphone.

Love many things, for therein lies the true strength, and whosoever loves much performs much, and can accomplish much, and what is done in love is done well.

She received an enthusiastic ovation. She looked over at us and smiled. Eve Weber would do great things. We would know Eve Weber for the rest of our lives. It was just our instinct.

Finally, Senator Jordan invited the club to the podium, along with Mr. Heinz and Miss Walsh. The Senator would introduce us, we would offer the found art as ownership to the Weber family, and Mr. Heinz would unveil the restored, cleaned Van Gogh art.

I spoke briefly.

"Since the moment we, the Young Climbers Club, cast our eyes on this remarkable work of art, our lives have not been the same. There were great days and *not*-so-great days." Most giggled as I rolled my eyes and smiled.

"One thing is for sure; we wouldn't change a moment of our adventure. We feel fortunate to have been the ones to find 'The Painter on His Way' to Work." Everyone applauded as I waited. "And so, it's with great pleasure and extreme gratification that we present this Vincent Van Gogh back to its family, now to its heirs. Accepting on behalf of her family is Eve Weber."

She joined us near the podium and hugged each club member. I nodded at Mr. Heinz, and he revealed a sight of beauty. The paint seemed to leap from the canvas. It was vibrant and took my breath away. Eve's expression was one of awe. She clasped her hands together and placed them over her heart. She looked upward and whispered, *"This is for you, Grandmama, with love."* She was speaking, of course, to the recently departed Ella Rosen Weber. There was a standing ovation as a sign of respect for art and the power of its presence. Eve and the family took their place next to the painting. Last, Senator Jordan awarded the club with a special plaque, recognizing the occasion.

"The words on this plaque are as heartfelt as any I've ever read."

The gentleman from the Bode Museum came and stood next to us. He didn't speak English very well, so he allowed the Senator to translate as he spoke.

"To the youth of our world who inspire us to do better, love better, and live better. To us, the people of Germany, we bestow the honorary title and well deserved To the Monuments Club."

My eyes popped out of their sockets. The gang all had the same expressions. What an honor. The place erupted in cheering and applause. We just grinned and continued taking bows and waving. *Huh, what a day.*

After what seemed like an hour, we were done doing interviews and taking pictures. Geez, we didn't think we'd get this much attention. It boggled our minds. Eve joined me and the gang as we wandered out to the garden for snacks and drinks.

CHAPTER THIRTY-THREE

We were feeling happy and laughing about this and that. Tula had been getting herself a drink at the table when my cell phone rang inside her purse. I'd forgotten it was there.

Eve excused herself for the moment. The gang and I huddled together because we were still laughing very hard at a Spooky comment. Shameful, I'm sure. I was still laughing when I hit the cell button.

"*Ha-ha*, hullo?"

I heard a young lady's voice on the other end. "Hello, is this Dean Mandel?" I tried to place her voice but couldn't, so I put it on speaker so the gang could help figure out who it might be. I answered the voice.

"Uh, yeah, I couldn't hear you. Can you repeat, please?" I shrugged as the gang leaned in to listen.

"Is this Dean Mandel?" Before I answered, she continued. "Dean Mandel, the leader of the Monuments Club?" The gang and I was shocked when we heard her questions. How could she even know that name in reference to their club?

"Who wants to know?" Tula furrowed her eyebrow indicating she didn't approve of my answer. "Eh, I mean, yes. Who am I speaking to?" I got Tula's wink of approval.

"I'm Jeanie Marlow. I lead the Canyon Bouldering Club a day or so north of you." Well, that added to the mystery. She was several hundred miles north, likely in the upper canyon area somewhere, I guessed.

"What can I, or the club, do for you?" I wasn't sure what else to say.

"Well." She paused, cautious for the right words, "We understand your club is the one who recovered the World War II Van Gogh painting. It's all over the newspapers, television, and Internet." She paused again. "We found something a week or so ago, and we didn't know where to turn."

We were more curious than ever.

"Well, what can we help you with? We don't know you, your club, where you are, or what you found."

"It's an artifact." I remained quiet for a moment. "I think you should see it. Call me on this number if you're interested. Thanks."

That was it. The caller hung up. She must think we know a lot about art or something. It sounded like she might have the wrong idea. For the record, we never even discussed changing the name of our club. I'm not sold on that.

Before the gang and I had a chance to chat about it, I looked across the garden and saw my father standing in the entryway, under the trellis, dressed in his uniform. He shook his head *no* to indicate that I shouldn't go to him. He gave the same look to Mom and Delilah, standing at the snack table.

He blew a kiss to us and made a heart with his hands. We'd already said our goodbyes earlier. My club fanned around me for support. I saluted him as he left and he returned the gesture, then he was gone. I looked at Mom, and she gave a thumbs up that she was okay. Boy, what an emotional day.

Before heading to the motorcade for our drive back to Flagstaff, the photographer waved at us. Two older distinguished gentlemen were admiring the painting around the security. We approached them. They were two of the nicest dudes we'd ever met.

They reminisced about World War II and the art and the ceremony. They introduced themselves only as Bernie and Rich. All they wanted was a photo of Eve, the gang, and themselves for a keepsake. Eve gave her blessing without pause. Meeting them made me appreciate what my father was off to do. I didn't know what, but it didn't matter, as long as he returned safely.

CHAPTER THIRTY-FOUR

The ride seemed short. I chilled out with my earbuds and music most of the way home. Tula and Jonas fell asleep, and Spooky rode in the Senator's car with his parents. There was only one more task for the day. We were ready to install Emily Davis. As we exited the cars, Spooky's Dad came over to extend his congratulations on a great day and a happy ending to a most excellent experience. As he turned to walk away, he asked about our last picture.

"By the way, did you run into Bernie and Rich?"

"Yes, they were nice dudes. They spent time telling us about World War II and their love of art. Are they friends of yours, Senator?" He seemed pleased that we met them.

"Me? Oh no. I met them today, too." He smiled before he continued. "I know they didn't mention to you who they were, did they?" We just looked at each other and shook our heads. "They were two of the remaining original members of the Monuments Men." We were in disbelief and didn't understand why they didn't introduce themselves to us that way.

"Senator, are you kidding? Why?"

"Because they didn't want to take the shine off you guys and Eve today. They left a way to reach out to them later if you wish. It was all about the art, your club, and Eve Weber today."

As the gang and I took it all in, meeting two Monuments Men made that day even more unbelievable.

The others and I changed into casual clothes and met at Home Base at 7:30. Emily arrived a few minutes later. We talked about our day. She mentioned she'd seen the television clips of the event. Finally, she took her oath before the Young Climber's Club members. We were blessed to have her in the club. Until that point, it'd only been the four of us. By the time school started again, we'd all be thirteen. We felt we needed to grow a little.

We handed her secret passwords, policies, which there were only a few, and our notes from the Van Gogh episode. It was a lot for a new member to take in, but Emily was a willing new member.

Well, there was nothing more to do but welcome Emily to the club. She went down our little receiving line and got a firm handshake and an enthusiastic welcome. Finally, she got to me.

"Well, Emily, it'll be our pleasure to have you with us. We consider you a valuable asset as well as a trustworthy team player. We're happy to have you as our new and hopefully long-time member."

I paused. The others were standing there, waiting for my final welcome. I looked at Tula. She raised her eyebrow. I glanced at Spooky, who wore his signature Cheshire cat grin. I peeked at Jonas, the mush ball. Yes, of course, he had a tear in his eye. Emily wore a pretty smile as she waited for the official call. I grinned my *best* Jack Nicholson grin.

"Emily, welcome to the Monuments Club."

About the Author

<u>Jan Eberle Schaberg</u> is and accomplished writer whose recent biography, Calm Waters, won first place at the National League of American Pen Women Conference. She is also the author of two children's books.

Jan also hosts a weekly radio show, The swing Museum on WWFM. The author is following in the footsteps of her father, Ray Eberle. She is into big band mu-sic, standards, and jazz and loves the music from the 1930s and 40s.

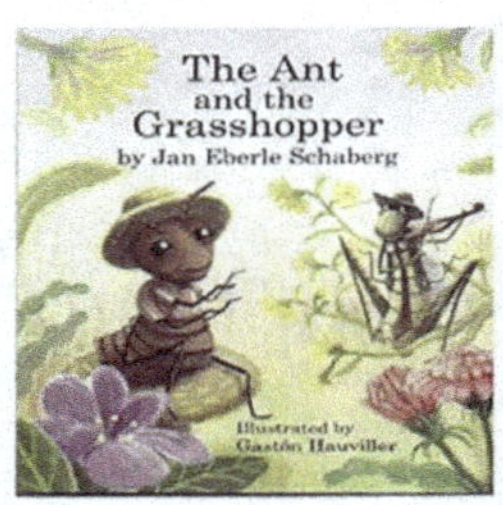

ACKNOWLEDGMENTS

Many thanks to the publisher, Brenda Spalding, for believing in **The Monuments Club.**

I also wish to thank my husband, Ray, for all he does to make things happen for me. He is the one constant in my life.